P9-EDO-116

"You have caused a great deal of trouble, Monsieur American Intelligence Agent," Avorix said.

"I will kill you long before you fire your weapon, Avorix. Please believe me," Carter said.

Something flashed in the man's eyes and Carter started to bring up his Luger, when Avorix's head snapped back as a sharp crack of an automatic came from the doorway.

Carter was around in a crouch, his Luger up and ready to fire before Avorix hit the floor.

Marie stood just within the doorway, her .380 Beretta in her right hand and a slight smile on her lips.

"Jesus H. Christ," Carter swore half to himself.

NICK CARTER IS IT!

"Nick Carter out-Bonds James Bond."
—Buffalo Evening News

"Nick Carter is America's #1 espionage agent."
—Variety

"Nick Carter is razor-sharp suspense."
—King Features

"Nick Carter is extraordinarily big."
—Bestsellers

"Nick Carter has attracted an army of addicted readers . . . the books are fast, have plenty of action and just the right degree of sex . . . Nick Carter is the American James Bond, suave, sophisticated, a killer with both the ladies and the enemy."
—The New York Times

FROM THE NICK CARTER
KILLMASTER SERIES

NICK CARTER

KILLMASTER

ZERO-HOUR STRIKE FORCE

CHARTER BOOKS, NEW YORK

"Nick Carter" is a registered trademark of The Condé Nast
Publications, Inc., registered in the United States Patent Office.

All characters in this book are fictitious.
Any resemblance to actual persons, living or dead,
is purely coincidental.

ZERO-HOUR STRIKE FORCE

A Charter Book/published by arrangement with
The Condé Nast Publications, Inc.

PRINTING HISTORY
Charter Original/March 1984

All rights reserved.
Copyright © 1984 by The Condé Nast Publications, Inc.
This book may not be reproduced in whole
or in part, by mimeograph or any other means,
without permission. For information address:
The Berkley Publishing Group,
200 Madison Avenue,
New York, New York 10016.

ISBN: 0-441-95935-0

Charter Books are published by The Berkley Publishing Group,
200 Madison Avenue, New York, New York 10016.
PRINTED IN THE UNITED STATES OF AMERICA

*Dedicated to the men of the
Secret Services of the United
States of America.*

PROLOGUE

The sun finally slipped below the horizon, and Bill Thompson, driving the company jeep, rubbed his tired eyes. It had been a miserable two hours so far out of Ras Tanura on the Persian Gulf, and they had another half hour yet before they would arrive at Aramco's Handley Marker 17 field.

There had been some sort of recurring trouble with the new System Seven pumps, and Riyadh was mad, Paris was mad, and—worst of all—New York had gotten hold of it, and Stewart M. Luise himself was mad.

"Listen, Bill, something has to be done out there," Thompson's boss, Mark Howard, chief of engineering in Paris, had told him.

"What am I supposed to do, go out there and hold the Saudi engineers' hands until they ask us to do something?"

"They've already asked. They want the best systems engineer we've got. You're it."

Thompson, a large man in his early fifties, sighed deeply, then nodded. He had done time in the Saudi oil fields, baked under the Kuwaiti sun, and eaten sand blown in from the United Arab Emirates, and he had hated every minute of it. The engineering section in Paris was more to his liking. The

1

kids could come over from the States a couple of times a year to visit. And in the summer when it got too hot in the city, he and Cheryl would hightail it to the mountains of Austria or Switzerland.

"This'll just be an in-and-quick-fix-then-out. I'm sure they're just screwing up somehow," Howard said.

"When do I leave?"

Howard grinned. "This afternoon, to Riyadh. Thad Barkley will meet you with the helicopter. He'll tag along out to the field."

"Barkley," Thompson said. The name rang a bell, but he couldn't quite place it.

"He's chief of security out there for us."

Thompson was startled. "Security? What the hell is going on out there, Mark? Why do we need security . . ." He hesitated in mid-sentence. "Thaddeus Barkley?" he said. "*General* Barkley?"

"You've heard of him," Howard replied. He didn't seem pleased.

"President Reagan fired him five or six months ago. Couldn't keep his mouth shut."

"He's the one. He worked for Westmoreland in Vietnam. Hell of a security man, from what I'm told. At any rate, he'll be waiting for you."

"What *is* going on out there?" Thompson asked again. But Howard had not been able to tell him a thing beyond the fact that a number of the System Seven pumps had been giving the field engineers trouble, and a systems man had been requested.

He had flown Paris to Cairo, where he had spent the night, and this morning he had flown to Riyadh, where Barkley had been waiting for him with the big Bell helicopter.

Barkley was seated now in the jeep's passenger seat, and Thompson glanced over at him. He was checking his watch again. He had been doing it all day, ever since they had left the Saudi capital city for the 250-mile flight out to the Gulf.

Barkley was a tall, thin man with a square jaw, gray hair cut very short, steel blue eyes, and a weathered complexion. He looked like a field commander, and except for his evident nervousness about something, he acted like one.

He had seemed genuinely surprised when Thompson had shown up, and had suggested that they remain in Riyadh for a couple of days to talk with the local engineers and go over field drawings.

"This is just going to be a quick in-and-out, Mr. Barkley," Thompson had said.

"Call me Thad," Barkley had said absently. "How quick is quick? A day?"

"A couple of hours."

Barkley had seemed somewhat relieved by that but had said nothing more on the flight out. Once they had reached Ras Tanura, the former general had insisted they leave for the field immediately. They would have been there and back by now, except that shortly after they had cleared the port city limits, they had had some trouble with the jeep—sand in the carburetor that Thompson had been able to fix.

They topped a rise, and in the distance below they could see the Aramco pumping field spreading for miles left and right, and well beyond the horizon to the west, the occasional gas relief flames lighting the darkening night sky like lonely beacons.

Thompson was always impressed, despite his years of work in the oil business, whenever he came upon such a sight. He automatically slowed down as he took it all in.

"What the hell are you doing?" Barkley snapped.

"What?" Thompson asked, surprised by the man's out-burst.

"You don't think I have the rest of my life to ferry you

around the desert, for Christ's sake! I want to be headed back to Riyadh tonight."

"What's the hurry? I thought you wanted time to study the problem—"

"You said a couple of hours was all it would take."

Thompson nodded.

"I'm going to hold you to it," Barkley said. He looked at his watch again. "It's just eight. We'll be there by eight-thirty. I'll expect you to be finished and ready to go no later than eleven-thirty. I'll drive on the way back."

Thompson was generally an easygoing man, but he had had just about all he could take of the ex-general's heavy-handed tactics.

"Just what the hell is going on out here, Barkley?"

Barkley jumped as if he had been stung. "What do you mean?"

"I want to know why the hell you had to tag along with me? What are you doing out here?"

"Looking out for America's interests," Barkley said quickly . . . too quickly. And Barkley's choice of words struck Thompson as odd. "Aramco's interests" he could understand. But why had the ex-general chosen to use "America's interests"?

"What's that supposed to mean?" Thompson asked.

"Just what it sounds like," Barkley said. He leaned a little closer. "Look, Thompson, you seem like the right sort. Out here in the desert it can get dangerous at times. You should know that; you've been in this business a hell of a lot longer than I have."

"There've been no Bedouin attacks on the fields or the pipelines for years."

"I'm talking about the Israelis. There's been talk . . ."

"What sort of talk?" Thompson asked, but Barkley just looked at him, tight-lipped, then he sat back and lit a cigarette. "What the hell are you getting at, Barkley?" Thompson demanded. But the former general would say no more.

Twenty minutes later they had made it down to the main gate, where they were passed through to the administration building.

Thompson climbed tiredly out of the jeep and went inside with Barkley. Habik Mazir-Sharif, the chief Saudi engineer for the site, was waiting for them in his office.

He jumped to his feet, a huge smile on his face. "Ah, Mr. Thompson, and Mr. Barkley, welcome to Handley Marker seventeen. I trust you had a not too unpleasant journey."

"It was fine, thanks," Thompson said. "I understand you're having trouble with the new System Seven pumps."

"But not at this moment, such a discussion," Mazir-Sharif, the diminutive engineer, said.

"What'd you say?" Barkley snapped.

The Saudi turned to him. "But first there is dinner awaiting us. You gentlemen have traveled far. Especially Mr. Thompson. You must be hungry."

"No—" Barkley started.

"Yes," Thompson said, interrupting.

"Very good." Mazir-Sharif grinned. He came around from behind his desk.

Barkley, who had been standing by the door, looked at Thompson and shook his head. "Shit," he said. He turned and hurried out of the office.

Thompson went after him, but by the time he had made it to where they had parked, the security chief had jumped in the jeep, had started the engine, and was heading down the main road toward the front gate.

"What the hell?" Thompson said half to himself.

Four Hercules C-130 air transport aircraft, flying very low

with no navigation lights, touched down for a landing eleven miles northwest of Aramco's Handley Marker 17 field. Within five minutes of their landing, four continuous-track desert transports, each hauling a low body trailer, headed toward the oil pumping site. The vehicles, like the aircraft, were marked with the blue and white Israeli Star of David.

It was late, around two in the morning, when the trouble siren blew, and Bill Thompson sat up in bed.

Barkley had left, deserting him, and he had decided to remain at the pumping station until morning, when he'd borrow another jeep and drive back to Ras Tanura.

He went to the window and looked outside. Far to the west he could see a series of flashes. He quickly got dressed and went out into the corridor, then ran down to administration at the far end of the main building.

Mazir-Sharif was there with a dozen other Saudis, and everyone was shouting at once.

"What is it?" Thompson demanded.

Mazir-Sharif, who had been screaming into the telephone, slammed the instrument down and looked up. "It was the Israelis," he said. "They attacked to the west, held numbers seven, thirteen, twenty-three, and forty-one for ten minutes, and then withdrew."

"The actual wellheads?" Thompson asked.

"Yes," Mazir-Sharif said. "And then they withdrew. Apparently to their airplanes."

"How far out are those wellheads?" Thompson asked.

"Seven is the nearest. It's five miles away."

"Let's go out there . . ." Thompson started to say, when a terrible rumbling began in the earth, and a moment later there was a tremendous white flash, and the building began coming down around them.

Thompson was dimly aware of three other flashes and shock waves within seconds of each other, and he found himself outside, hanging on to what was left of Mazir-Sharif's right arm. In the distance, to the far west, the night sky was a roiling mass of flame. But he could see, rising up out of the burning cauldron, four classically formed mushroom clouds. *The Israelis,* he thought just before the fire storm of molten sand and rock buried him, *finally did it. . . .*

ONE

Nick Carter came up from Lafayette Square on Connecticut Avenue in the bumper-to-bumper traffic. It was crazy, but it seemed as if half the country had converged on Washington, D.C., within twenty-four hours of the attack on the oil fields of Saudi Arabia. Special interest groups from ban-the-bombers to the Ku Klux Klan, and from the Knights of Columbus to the Jewish Anti-Defamation League, all wanted their opinions heard.

"This is the eve of the end of the world," one sign on Pennsylvania Avenue read.

"Hiroshima, Nagasaki, the Saudi oil fields . . . are we next?" read another.

"Israel 4, Saudi Arabia 0," still another proclaimed.

Carter had been in El Salvador for the past three weeks as an observer, and as soon as the nuclear attack on the oil fields west of Dammam had hit the world press, he had hurried back to Washington.

That had been three days ago. Even using his military priority credentials it had taken him that long to fly out to Miami and then up to Washington, where he had picked up his car from storage at the airport.

He was dead tired now, this afternoon, but from the headlines in the papers, and from what he was hearing on the radio, there wasn't going to be much time for sleep in the very near future.

The traffic cleared for a moment near M Street, and Carter shot ahead, making it the next few blocks up to Dupont Circle and the headquarters of Amalgamated Press and Wire Services—the front for AXE, the United States' ultrasecret intelligence agency—in a couple of minutes.

He swung the turbo-charged Porsche into the underground garage, where he showed his credentials, then took the elevator up to Operations and again flashed his ID.

The place was a madhouse, and no one seemed to notice Carter as he crossed the ready room and ducked into his office. He had just lit a cigarette when his telephone rang.

"Carter," he said.

"N3, Hawk would like to see you immediately."

It was David Hawk's secretary, Ginger Bateman. Hawk was the hard-bitten chief of AXE. He was one of the few people on this earth for whom Carter had a genuine respect. When the man said jump, *everyone* jumped. Even presidents held Hawk in respect.

"On my way," Carter said into the telephone, but Ginger had already hung up. He put the phone down, took a deep drag on his cigarette and stubbed it out, then went back across Operations to the rear elevator that took him up to the fifth floor.

Once again he had to show his credentials before he was allowed down the corridor and into Hawk's outer office. Carter could rarely remember security being so tight.

Hawk's secretary waved him through, and he stepped into Hawk's inner sanctum, closing the door softly behind him and crossing the room to the large, cluttered desk.

David Hawk, an older man, short and stocky with a bulldoglike neck and a thick shock of white hair, was bent over some paperwork, a half-chewed cigar in his mouth, and he just waved Carter to a seat.

He seemed harried. His coat was off, his tie was loose, and his sleeves were rolled up.

Three television sets in the corner were switched on to network news programs, but the sound was turned off. Carter glanced over at one. A map of Saudi Arabia showed the four nuclear strikes, and a moment later a larger map, this one of the entire region, showed a red-dotted path from Israel to Saudi Arabia.

"I'm sending you over," Hawk said, bringing Carter around.

"Sir?"

"To Riyadh, with the President's negotiating team. You'll be part of the implementation coordination team. Should give you plenty of freedom to move around."

"I don't quite understand, sir."

"I want you over there, in Saudi Arabia, to find out what the hell happened."

"It was my understanding that the Israelis made the strike."

"Israeli-marked aircraft—four Hercules—and Israeli-marked ground transport. Uzi machine guns. A couple of dead soldiers with Israeli identification. A little too obvious."

"To be expected if the Israelis actually made the attack."

"On four oil wells? They killed several dozen people, among them one American oil engineer. They contaminated a large oil field. And they ruined a lot of pumping equipment. Beyond that—nothing. And I mean absolutely *nothing*, except you've got to consider that they've incited the entire Arab world into a frenzy of war fever."

"I see, sir," Carter said, and he was beginning to see. It didn't make much sense. Whenever the Israelis attacked, they did so decisively. If they had wanted to attack Saudi Arabia—and with nuclear weapons—they would have at least gone for Riyadh, the capital city, and some of the oil port towns. Not just four oil wells.

"Begin personally denied that the Israelis had anything whatsoever to do with the attack. He has no idea where the aircraft came from or, more importantly, where the nuclear devices were produced."

"It does narrow the field, doesn't it, sir?" Carter said. "The Russians?"

"Possibly," Hawk said. He sat back in his chair. "The President has condemned the attack, and yesterday he offered to send a peace-keeping and investigatory force over there. Both Israel and Saudi Arabia agreed immediately."

"What about the Soviet Union? I haven't heard what they've had to say about it."

"They've not said a thing, Nick. Not one word. Which is beginning to worry a lot of people. The President has ordered our military on DEFCON two, something that's not been done since the Cuban missile crisis."

"The Soviets have responded in kind?"

Hawk nodded. "Our people are going over to Riyadh for show, mostly. If we can keep everyone talking, for a few days at least, the President hopes the situation will defuse itself."

"That's not likely."

"No," Hawk said. "If they had used conventional weapons, yes . . . perhaps. But not with nuclear devices. There's too much hysteria. And it's building, Nick. Building in a very bad way. Slowly, deeply."

Hawk got up and went across the room to the sideboard where he poured them both a stiff shot of bourbon. He brought the drinks back and perched on the edge of his desk.

"Smitty will give you your briefing, and we're working

out your background. You'll be a State Department employee. Rather low-level. No one will be paying much attention to you. The Central Intelligence Agency has worked out some of the details already. They think they may have a handle on where the aircraft originated. I want you to contact them. Smitty will give you the details. But we're not going to depend on the Company. I don't think there's enough time.''

Carter took a deep drink of the bourbon and lit a cigarette. He wasn't liking this very much. Taking on an individual, or even an organization, was one thing. Taking on an entire country was an entirely different matter.

''You're going to have to do this in a few days if we're going to be able to defuse the situation. I want you in there. I want you to find out where the aircraft and equipment came from, whose troops were used, and—most importantly— who supplied the nuclear devices and why only that oil field was hit.''

''Then what?'' Carter asked. His N3 Killmaster designation was his license to kill in the line of duty. But who did you take a shot at when an entire country was involved, with nuclear war at stake?

''We'll have to deal with your 'Then what?' when we get to it. Providing we get to it in time.''

Carter finished his drink, set the glass down, and got to his feet. At the door he hesitated. ''Have you any hunches, sir? Any guesses?''

''A lot of them, Nicholas,'' Hawk said not unkindly. ''But I'll keep them to myself for the moment. I want you over there fresh.'' They looked at each other for a long moment. There were times when their relationship was almost that of a father and son. There were other times, like now, when Carter could not fathom his boss.

The moment passed, and Carter left Hawk's office, taking

the elevator down to Operations where Howard Schmidt, known as Smitty, was waiting by the door to his office. He was another bulldog of a man, short, stocky—an ex-field man type. What he didn't know about intelligence service field work wasn't worth knowing. He didn't look particularly happy.

"You're leaving with the presidential team on Air Force One at 0400. We have a lot of ground to cover before then."

Carter glanced at his watch. It was just a few minutes before four, which left him a scant twelve hours before he'd be leaving for Riyadh. He had been on tighter schedules before, and certainly on more complicated missions. But this one did not seem right. Something seemed out of kilter to Carter. He wasn't psychic, but he had developed that sixth sense that comes from years of experience. The alarms were ringing all over the place for him now.

"My suitcases are downstairs in my car. Send someone over to my apartment with them, to repack," Carter said. He gave his keys to Smitty, who nodded. "I'll need a complete list of who will be going over on the negotiating team. And it'll have to be the real backgrounds. I don't want any surprises."

Again Smitty nodded. They walked across Operations. Smitty gave Carter's apartment keys to one of the young staffers, then they continued to the elevators.

"I'll need the rundown on CIA operations not only in and around Riyadh, but in the entire Middle East as well. I don't want any surprises there either. Especially not there."

The elevator came, and they took it down to the subbasement well below the parking levels where the computer archives, communications equipment, and briefing areas for ultrasensitive projects were located. It almost seemed to Carter that he had spent half his life either coming from this place or heading toward it.

"We'll begin with the negotiating team," Smitty said as they entered a briefing room. Several other people from Operations and Archives were waiting for them. It was going to be a long session. But the more information Carter got here, before he began, the easier his job would be, so he seldom if ever gave anything less than his best at these sessions.

Carter was driven over to a side entrance at the State Department on 23rd Street a little before 3:00 A.M., where he was met by Bob Sutherland, an undersecretary of state for Middle Eastern affairs.

They shook hands. "No one else on the team will know exactly who you are, Mr. Carter," Sutherland said. He was tall, well built, and had a pleasant face.

"I'll be working for you?" Carter asked. They went down the long first-floor corridor, their heels echoing loudly.

"That's right. I'll be able to cover for you—up to a point."

They stopped by the stairs down to the garage.

"To a point, Mr. Carter, and that's all," Sutherland said. "You have to understand that I'll be trying to work this out as best I can with the others on the team."

"I understand. And I appreciate your being up front with me. As long as we can continue that way, there'll be no problem."

Sutherland laughed as they started down. "No problem? On the contrary, Mr. Carter, we have ourselves one hell of a big problem."

At the bottom, they went through a thick steel door out into the parking garage. A dozen or more people were getting into limousines for the drive to Andrews Air Force Base. No one paid Sutherland or Carter much attention, although Carter was introduced to a number of people.

Smitty had assured him that there would be no Company

people aboard this trip, and only one State Department intelligence officer: Sutherland.

A police escort was waiting for them as they emerged from the State Department garage and turned left toward Constitution Avenue. They sped up going through the nearly deserted streets, and within a minute or two had passed the Elipse and the Capitol.

Sutherland and Carter were in the last limousine, alone. Behind them were two police cars. The limo's telephone buzzed, and Sutherland reached forward and picked it up.

"Sutherland," he said softly. A moment later the expression on his face changed. "Yes, Mr. President, I understand." He glanced at Carter. "Yes, sir, he is seated right next to me."

Sutherland handed the telephone to Carter. "The President would like to speak with you."

"Good morning, Mr. President," Carter said.

"I spoke with David Hawk a little while ago. He assures me that you are the man for the job, Mr. Carter."

"Thank you for the confidence, sir. I hope it's not misplaced."

"I sincerely hope not. But I wanted to reach you this morning before you got out to Andrews to tell you that if there is anything . . . anything at all that you might need, you will have it if it is within my power and the power of the United States to give it to you. Do you understand?"

"Yes, Mr. President."

The President was silent for a moment, apparently expecting Carter to give him some reassurances. But when nothing came he cleared his throat. "Well then, good luck to you."

"Thank you, sir," Carter said, and he replaced the telephone in its console.

Sutherland was looking at him with new respect. "I have a

feeling, Carter, that I don't know who you really are. Nor, do I suspect, will you fill me in.''

"You're batting a thousand, Bob. Just give me a little cover over there, and I'll see what I can come up with.''

Sutherland's gaze moved to the telephone and then back again to Carter. He smiled and shook his head. "Whatever you say.''

The caravan turned down 1st Street past the Library of Congress, then took Pennsylvania Avenue all the way down across the river and went out old Highway 4 to the interstate, finally turning south again to the west gate into Andrews.

Carter had been mildly surprised that they had not taken the Capital Beltway out. They also had not used the main gate. It wasn't likely that anyone knew they'd be leaving at this hour, nor was it likely that anyone would be out here to see them off.

He was about to tell Sutherland just that when he noticed Air Force One sitting on the ramp in front of Base Operations. What he noticed at the same moment was a very large crowd of people surging back and forth behind barricades that the military police had set up. As the car got closer he could see that there were at least two hundred military cops who were just barely able to hold back the crowd. There were a lot of signs, and Carter could hear the crowd chanting something.

"Oh, shit,'' Sutherland said, and he picked up the phone. "Unit one, this is eight. We'd better go around to the far side of the bird. Less exposure.''

The lead limousine and police escort swung left, going behind the big presidential jet, so that the aircraft was between them and the crowd.

Something flew out of the crowd, landing on the tarmac with a large red splash. Immediately a dozen cops leaped over the barriers and waded into the crowd.

The first of the negotiating team were already out of their limousines and hurrying around to the boarding steps when Carter and Sutherland pulled up and got out.

The morning was warm and very humid, the smell of jet fuel strong, the jumbled noise of the immense crowd awesome. There were a lot of reporters, TV cameras, and photographers on the other side of the barrier, but they were apart from the mob. They were taking pictures of the departing delegates as well as the crowd.

Sutherland had a walkie-talkie pressed to his lips, and he was issuing a rapid-fire stream of orders as he and Carter ducked under the plane and came around to the boarding stairs.

Another roar went up from the crowd, and a large number of the people began chanting: "No more war! No more war! No more war!"

A few microphones had been hastily set up at the foot of the stairs, and Assistant Secretary of State Howard Huntington and Phillipe Hermande, a special adviser to the President on Middle Eastern affairs, were speaking with several media people who had been let through the barrier.

"Christ," Sutherland swore. He hurried around to the front of the aircraft and gave the pilot the signal to start his engines.

Then he started back to Huntington. All of a sudden a large rock sailed through the air from the crowd, landing just a few feet away from the microphones.

Huntington stopped his speech and stepped back, a confused, almost hurt expression on his face.

Carter was on his other side.

"I think we'd better get on the plane, sir," Carter said.

Huntington looked from him to Sutherland, who had just raced up.

"He's right, Mr. Secretary. The crowd will break through those barriers at any moment."

The news people were photographing and filming the exchange. Huntington had started to say something when the first of the four jet engines whined into life, making conversation all but impossible.

The crowd roared, the noise audible even over the second engine that had started up.

Carter looked back as the front line of military cops went down under the surge of a thousand people.

Sutherland saw it at the same moment, and he and Carter grabbed Huntington by the arms and literally lifted him off his feet and hustled him up the boarding stairs.

Hermande had already scrambled inside.

At the top they were suddenly pelted with rocks, but then they were in, and the steward slammed the hatch closed.

Sutherland ducked onto the flight deck, shouting, "Go! Go!"

Immediately the big plane lurched to the right, and they began to move as the last of the jet engines started.

"Get everyone strapped in, Nick. We're getting out of here now," Sutherland shouted.

Carter helped Huntington back to his seat and made sure everyone had his seat belt on, then he took a seat near an emergency exit over the wing as they accelerated down the taxiway toward the main north-south runway.

Behind them were thousands of people gone crazy. In the distance, Carter could see several fire trucks and a half-dozen troop transports racing to the riot. But no one was trying to follow Air Force One. One fanatic with a gun would have been all it would have taken.

They finally turned onto the main runway, held there for a few moments, then started their takeoff roll.

Carter relaxed back in his seat as he watched the runway

lights flashing by, and then they were lifting off, Washington, D.C., and its surrounding suburbs spreading out to the north.

He wondered what their reception would be like in Riyadh.

TWO

Riyadh had always been an important oasis city in a desert area of Saudi Arabia known as Nejed. To the south was the fearsome desert of Rub' al Khali. To the north the Arma Plateau. And to the west and east the troubled Red Sea and the important Persian Gulf.

The city itself was not very large, less than a quarter of a million people, and was a blend of the ancient and of the ultramodern.

For years the city had been the natural stopping place on the camel caravan trade routes. Ancient bazaars, minarets, and a rat's maze of narrow alleys and side streets had the flavor of any Arab city.

But with the new oil wealth came the television towers, glass and steel skyscrapers, and ultramodern hotels that catered to the visitor's every wish except one. No liquor was served in the city, nor, for that matter, anywhere in the country . . . legally.

The trip across the Atlantic to Paris, where they refueled, was uneventful. Carter caught up on his sleep, Huntington spent most of the time on the encrypted telephone line to the President, and most of the others, including Sutherland, played poker.

At least two hundred thousand people ringed the Charles de Gaulle Airport outside of Paris, but the gendarmes had the situation well in hand, and the nearest the crowd ever came to Air Force One as she refueled was three quarters of a mile away.

Cairo, where they made their second stop, was deserted except for the soldiers who instantly surrounded the aircraft and remained with it until it took off an hour after it landed.

It was 4:30 P.M., Washington time—1:30 A.M. the following morning local time—when they approached Riyadh from the northwest.

Sutherland had gone forward to talk with the crew, and Carter had been sitting by the window eating his dinner and having a drink.

There was nothing below them except the dark desert in every direction, so Carter was surprised when the seat belt sign flashed on and they began their descent.

Sutherland came back and sat down next to Carter.

"We'll be on the ground in ten minutes."

Carter looked out the window again but still could not see anything. It suddenly occurred to him that Saudi Arabia had been attacked, the country would be on a war footing, and there would of course be a blackout.

"Any word on our reception?" Carter asked.

Sutherland shrugged. "They're expecting us. They gave us the nod when the President suggested this trip. And we'll be treated as visiting diplomats, of course. But if you mean will the brass bands and cheering crowds be there to greet us, don't count on it."

"I meant our freedom. Will we be allowed to come and go?"

"I don't know, Nick. But I seriously doubt it. The best I'll be able to do for you is set you up in whatever hotel they give us so that you can get out of there without being spotted."

"Have there been any restrictions on Americans' movements within the country?"

"Not yet that I know of," Sutherland replied. "Of course our embassy is mobbed. There are a lot of our people who want to get the hell out of here. And the President has ordered the wives and families of all our people home. But that's less out of fear of some kind of retaliation from the Saudis than it is from fear that Riyadh will be attacked next."

Carter glanced out the window at the darkness below. Suddenly a wide path outlined by white lights appeared in front of them. The runway had been lit up. Within sixty seconds they touched down, and two minutes later, the runway lights once again extinguished, they were following the taillights of a dimly lit truck along the taxiway to the terminal.

A huge tarpaulin flapped in the early morning breeze in front of the terminal building, and Air Force One just eased beneath it, then stopped, its jet engines cutting off and winding down.

Several dozen soldiers in full battle dress stood in formation outside the terminal, and as Carter continued to watch out the window, at least a hundred more soldiers quickly surrounded the airplane.

A dozen men, all dressed in traditional Arab robes, came out of the terminal and stood stiffly waiting as a set of boarding steps was brought into position.

Assistant Secretary Huntington strode to the front of the airplane and motioned for the steward to hold off opening the main hatch for just a moment. Everyone looked expectantly up at him.

"Saudi Arabia considers itself at war, as you all can imagine. While we are here we will conduct ourselves at all times as American diplomats sensitive to the very grave issues facing this oil-rich section of real estate."

There was some scattered applause, but Huntington held up his hands for silence.

"We have a few ground rules which we'll have to abide by while we're here," he said, and Carter suddenly got a very uncomfortable feeling that the bottom was going to drop out of his plans.

"I have been in radio contact over the past hour with Sheik ali-Fassam, assistant minister of defense, who presented only two conditions to our arrival. The first is that we will be escorted wherever we go. We'll be staying at the Sheraton downtown. Lovely hotel. I was there just four months ago." Huntington paused a moment. "And the second will be nothing more than a minor inconvenience; our luggage as well as our persons will be searched upon exiting the aircraft."

There were a number of groans.

"I have been assured that it will be done with a minimum of fuss and in a very subdued manner. Our papers will not be disturbed, nor will our personal things. They merely want to assure themselves that we are carrying in no secret transmitters, nor are we carrying in any weapons."

Sutherland, who had gone up next to Huntington, whispered something in his ear. Huntington seemed startled, and then he shook his head. Sutherland tried again, but again Huntington shook his head. "Unthinkable . . ." Carter heard the single word clearly.

Sutherland came back to where Carter was sitting. The steward opened the door, and Huntington, Hermande, and their immediate aides all stepped outside.

"No dice, Nick," Sutherland said.

"He knows about me, doesn't he?" Carter asked. He watched out the window as Huntington was greeted, and then a man in Western clothes quickly frisked him and Hermande. Carter was having a hard time believing what he was seeing.

Diplomats searched? But then Saudi Arabia had been attacked with nuclear weapons.

"Yes, technically, but he'd rather not have to think about you or deal with you in any way. If you have weapons, he told me to tell you to leave them aboard the aircraft."

"We won't be searched?"

"The aircraft won't be."

"Then I'm staying aboard," Carter said.

Sutherland was startled. "How the hell are you going to get anything done . . ." he began, but then he cut it off. He smiled. "Let me guess. You want me to bring you a robe and headdress."

It was a thought. But Carter smiled. "No, thanks, Bob. I don't want your position jeopardized. Besides, I've got to get out of here tonight. We can't afford to drag this out."

"Then how . . . ?"

"That's my problem. You got me here. The rest is up to me." The plane had emptied, and it was time for Sutherland to go. "Stick with Huntington. He's going to need all the help he can get."

Sutherland got up and looked toward the forward hatch. "This is his big chance, politically."

"Don't let him screw it up. I need time."

"Good luck," Sutherland said.

He and Carter shook hands, and then he left with the others. The steward came back.

"Aren't you leaving, sir?" he asked.

"Nope," Carter said, getting up. "What I want you to do is close and lock that forward hatch, and then ask the captain to come back here."

"Yes, sir," the steward said crisply. He went forward, closed and locked the main hatch, then disappeared onto the flight deck.

Carter poured himself a drink from the aft galley, and a

couple of minutes later the captain came back. Carter poured him a drink as well.

"Charlie says you're staying aboard?" the captain asked. He was an Air Force major.

"Just until things quiet down," Carter said. "How about you and the crew?"

"We'll be leaving in a half hour or so. We have to stick with the off-loading of the luggage."

"You'll seal the hatches when you leave?"

"That's right. No one will be able to get in or out."

Carter smiled. "You don't seal the wheel wells."

"Impossible with the wheels down . . ." the captain said, but then he understood. "The access panel."

"It was an alternative I discussed with my boss."

"Whose name I have no interest in knowing," the captain said. He tossed his drink back. "Good luck, Carter, and I sincerely mean that. A lot is riding on what happens out here in the next couple of days."

"You might pass the word along to Bob Sutherland, but to no one else."

"Yes, sir," the captain said, and he went forward again.

The steward came back. "Is there anything I can do for you, sir, before we deplane?"

"Yes, I want all the window shades closed."

"Of course, sir."

Carter remained in the galley area as the steward worked his way forward, sliding down the opaque plastic window shades on both sides. He returned to the galley.

"There'll be no electrical power, nor will there be any light or water pressure, sir," the man said.

"Don't worry, I'll be fine," Carter said. "Just go do your job and forget you ever saw me or heard of me."

The steward nodded. "Good luck, sir," he said.

Carter poured himself another drink and nudged open the

door that led into the President's aft sleeping quarters. It looked almost like a motel room except the bedspread was a violent blue with the presidential seal in the middle. A private bathroom was tucked in the forward bulkhead.

He closed the door and went back into the main cabin where he sat down, lit a cigarette, and crossed his legs. He uncrossed them. He'd have to remember that in Saudi Arabia, to cross one's legs meant disrespect. Strange, some of their customs.

Twenty minutes later, the flight captain came to the forward galley and looked back. "We're opening the hatch now and leaving. The master switch is off."

The copilot and navigator came out of the flight deck. Both stewards stood there as well.

Carter raised his drink in salute.

"I left the access hatch undogged. You'll have to crawl back to the main gear well. It'll be easier."

"Thanks," Carter said.

"Well," the captain said. "Good luck."

The main hatch was opened, and Carter could instantly hear the sounds of the airport; a large air conditioner was running somewhere, and someone was shouting in Arabic. He could also feel the heat of the desert. Then the hatch was closed again.

For a half hour afterward, Carter listened in the darkness to the sounds of the luggage being taken out of the compartments below, but then those hatches were closed and sealed, and he sat in pitch-dark silence.

He took out his penlight and quietly opened the overhead luggage rack, where he had stowed his single suitcase. From inside he took out his two extra passports, one a German passport, the other British. Both were well used, filled with visas and stamps from around the world. He pocketed these, as well as several thousand dollars in Saudi riyals and five small packets each containing ten thousand dollars' worth of diamonds. The diamonds did not come out of AXE's budget, Smitty had explained. They had been part of a payment on a very large drug bust that was shared with AXE through government channels.

He would have liked to have taken the suitcase with him, but a man in Western dress wandering around Riyadh in the middle of the night was going to be suspicious enough without it.

He looked at his watch. It was well after 2:00 A.M. He sat down by a window on the side opposite the terminal and switched off his penlight. He touched his left side with his left elbow. Wilhelmina, his 9mm Luger, was there. He could feel, Hugo, his pencil-thin stiletto, on his right forearm, and encased in a special pouch high on his left thigh was Pierre, his specially designed gas bomb.

When he felt his eyes were fully adjusted to the darkness, he carefully eased the window shade up about half an inch, then hunched down so he could peer outside.

At first he could see nothing, but then he picked out a pair of soldiers in a jeep, well forward, and aft there was another jeep, this one with a single soldier seated behind the wheel, his partner leaning against the hood.

There was nothing else out there other than darkness in the direction of the taxiways and runway. Only a small amount of illumination from the terminal on the other side of the plane shone any light on the tarmac.

Carter closed the plastic shade and moved to the other side of the aircraft. If anyone were watching the plane, he would be on this side. Carter realized he would have to be very careful; to be discovered at this point would effectively end his mission.

Slowly he raised the shade just a fraction of an inch, barely far enough for him to look beneath it. There was no one there.

The boarding stairs had been trundled away, the guards who had been lined up near the main terminal doors when the plane first arrived were gone, and Carter could see clearly into the terminal. He saw no one.

He closed the shade and sat back in the darkness. The plane was sealed. They'd have no reason to suspect anyone was aboard. They'd only be watching for intruders, someone trying to get *in*, not someone trying to get *out*.

He waited for another half hour, then got up and by feel worked his way forward, where he opened the door to the flight deck. The jeep with the two soldiers inside was visible just forward of the nose, and he ducked down below the level of the windshield.

Above and to the left, between the tarpaulin and the roof-line, he could see the control tower rising above the terminal. But anyone there wouldn't be able to see him down here. Not at that distance, with this poor light.

The square plate in the deck, just behind the pilot's and copilot's seats, was loose, all six fasteners out.

He pulled open the plate and looked down inside the bowels of the aircraft. An access passageway ran for most of the length of the plane. He eased down into it, closed the access plate over his head, then switched on his penlight.

It was very hot down here, and it smelled of kerosene and oil. Hydraulic lines and electrical cables ran back and forth through the narrow tunnel.

He slowly worked his way aft, careful to make absolutely no noise that anyone outside would be able to hear. Sweat covered his face despite the fact that the desert air was not humid.

An access plate just below him was marked LUGGAGE COMPARTMENT 1P. Another access hatch, on the opposite side of the narrow catwalk, was marked LUGGAGE COMPARTMENT 1S. One port and one starboard.

He continued toward the rear of the plane, eventually coming to another set of luggage compartment hatches. Finally he saw a pair of wider hatches marked LANDING MAINS port and starboard.

The starboard side was toward the terminal, the port, away. The portside access hatch was loose. Shining his penlight on the fasteners, he could see that they had been unscrewed. The captain or one of his crewmen had crawled down here and undone the hatch for him, figuring this was his only way out.

Carter decided that Hawk would hear about this. It would be passed on to the President and would come down to the crew's files.

He switched off the penlight and sat back against a bulkhead support while he waited for his eyes to adjust to the darkness.

Five minutes later he eased down off the catwalk between the maze of wiring and plumbing, and lifted the access hatch up and to the left.

Immediately the hot smells of the tarmac wafted up to him. The very large landing gear was directly beneath him, beyond a network of tubing, struts, hydraulic lines, and other unidentifiable parts.

Carter eased himself down into the gear well, closing the hatch behind him. He worked his way down through the maze until he was crouched atop the outboard wheel, then he slipped down between the pair of tires.

Forward, Carter could see the jeep just beyond the nose of the aircraft. Beyond the jeep was the edge of the terminal building. Aft, the other jeep was parked beyond the tail section. But to the right, just beyond the starboard wing and hidden in shadow, was the end of the terminal.

Carter's trousers and jacket were dark. It would be an iffy

proposition whether or not the guards in the aft jeep would see him if he scurried beneath the wing and around the corner of the building.

He waited for several minutes, watching the jeep just off the tail, until the flare of a match lit up the interior of the vehicle.

Without hesitation he ducked around the wheels and, keeping low, raced beneath the wing and across the open space to the shadows at the edge of the long, narrow terminal building.

For a few crucial seconds after the soldier had struck a match to light his cigarette, he and his companion had totally lost their night vision.

Carter hurried around the corner of the building, which fronted into a service entrance. He hurried around the edge of the service area, then climbed up over a large trash bin and a tall cement block barrier just beyond it.

He hung at the edge for several moments until he was sure no one was watching, then he jumped down to the wide sidewalk that led back up to the front of the terminal where taxis waited and the passenger bus into town picked up its passengers for the various hotels.

At the first of the main doors, he ducked inside. Only two of the ticket counters were manned, and there were only a few people in the terminal. He made a U-turn to the far doors and casually stepped outside and across the wide sidewalk to the pair of cabs waiting.

Both drivers were asleep, so Carter got into the back seat of the lead cab and slammed the door. The driver came instantly awake.

"*Salaam alaykum*," Carter said.

"*Wa alaykum essalaam*," the driver responded automatically.

It was nearly the extent of Carter's spoken Arabic, but it had worked. The driver started the cab, and they headed away from the airport.

Although it was three in the morning, there was quite a bit of traffic on the main highway. Army trucks and jeeps hurried back and forth, and every intersection was sandbagged.

The driver, once he woke up, studied Carter's reflection in the rearview mirror. He did not look too happy about carrying someone who obviously was an American or European.

"Where you wish to go?" the driver asked in English.

"*Bitte?*" Carter said. He did not want the cabby reporting to the police or the military authorities that he had taken an American from the airport well after all the other Americans had gotten off the plane.

"You're German?" the driver asked in German.

"*Ja,*" Carter said. He gave the driver an address in the residential district several blocks west of the big soccer stadium downtown.

"We cannot go that way, mein Herr," the driver said. "We will have to go around to the south first."

"What's the problem?"

"The stadium has been taken over by the military. Prisoners are being kept there."

Carter took out a cigarette and lit it. "Then let's stay away from the stadium, my friend. Just get me to Mar-es-Salaam without trouble. I wish no trouble."

"Nor I, mein Herr," the cabby said.

THREE

The cabby dropped Carter off at the corner of Ras Hanna, and after Carter had made sure it was out of sight, he hurried several blocks deeper into Mar-es-Salaam, to the Central Intelligence Agency's operational safe house Smitty had told him about. The Company ran its business out of the embassy, of course, but for particularly delicate operations, the safe house was used. Even the ambassador did not know about it.

"You'll have to work with them on this one, Nick," Smitty had cautioned him. "There are no AXE operations in Saudi Arabia, not since Owen was killed."

Owen, Carter vaguely remembered, had run a very small watchdog operation here in Riyadh until he was killed in an automobile accident in 1973. Before anything could be done to cover his background, the Saudi police had gone to his apartment where they had found passport-making equipment, a gun with ammunition, and other incriminating evidence that proved Owen was an American spy. The story had been kept out of the papers, but President Nixon had promised the Saudi government that whoever Owen had worked for would not set up shop again. And except for special operations, AXE had remained out of the country.

Carter stood in the darkness across the street from the tall cement block wall that separated the courtyard and house from its neighbors.

He was very conscious of the passage of time and of the fact that if anything was to be done yet tonight, under the protection of darkness, it would have to begin very soon. It was well after 3:00 A.M. In a few hours the dawn would come.

He had gone around the block once to check for any surveillance units but had found nothing. If there had been the time, he would have done it again, just to make sure. But he was going to have to take a lot of chances on this one if he was going to get anything done in the very short time allotted. The situation over here was on a very short fuse, and nuclear war was at the other end.

Once across the street, he rang the bell beside the thick wooden gate. He could just barely hear it from well within.

Almost immediately a small opening at eye level was shoved back.

"I'm Carter," he said.

The door was opened and he was allowed inside by a tall, very husky man dressed in the traditional Arab robes. He was an American.

"Welcome to the hot seat. I'm Carl Eklund," he said.

They shook hands, and Eklund led him across a wide, pleasant courtyard and into the house, which was dark.

"We have to watch out for our neighbors. We can't be anything more than what we pretend to be . . . just one big happy Saudi family," Eklund said.

They went to the back of the house, then inside a large room that was lit with red lights. A woman in Arab dress, her veil pushed aside and her long skirt pulled up to her lovely thighs, was strapping a pistol to her right leg.

She looked up. "How'd you get past the airport reception?" she asked, finishing what she was doing.

"I waited until they were gone, then snuck out the back way."

"The back way?" the woman said, dropping the hem of her dress and straightening up.

"Trade secret."

"Mr. Carter, Joy Makepiece, our chief of station," Eklund said.

They shook hands. "And I don't want to hear any cracks about my legs, my gender, or Mata Hari. I've heard them all."

She turned to Eklund. "Are you ready to go, Carl?"

He nodded. "They should have something by now."

She turned back to Carter. "If you want to tag along, you'll have to dress in a *ghutra* and *thobe*. You can put them over your street clothes. Although if you want my advice, Mr. Carter, you should go back to the hotel with your State Department pals."

"I don't want your advice, Miss Makepiece . . . or Mrs. . . . or Ms. . . . and I came here with a job to do that does not include sitting around a conference table."

Her nostrils flared and her right eyebrow rose. Eklund tossed him a white robe and headpiece, which he quickly donned over his street clothes.

"Where are we going, and who should have something by now?" Carter asked.

Joy had gone to the window, and she shoved the heavy curtains aside just far enough so that she could see outside.

"There are four of us working out of the embassy here," Eklund explained. "The other two are Brent Williams and Laila Haddab . . . she's a local."

Joy turned back. "It's clear. We've been chasing after a small but very well-organized terrorist group for about six months now. They've been operating, for some reason, here in Saudi Arabia and to a lesser extent, we're told, in Israel. But we think they may be funded by Kaddafi.''

"Do you think they had some connection with the nuclear strike?''

"I don't know. But it's our only lead at the moment, and I mean only.''

"We think several of their leaders were arrested in the roundup,'' Eklund said.

"And they're being held at the soccer stadium?''

"That's right,'' Joy said. "Brent and Laila managed to get themselves arrested and into the stadium. By now we're hoping they'll have cornered one or more of the top three: Jarabub, Malindi, and Beylia. They call themselves the July Committee.''

"And we're getting into the stadium this morning?'' Carter asked.

"That's right,'' Joy said. "But you don't have to tag along.''

Carter looked at his watch. "We don't have much darkness left. If we're going to do it, let's get on with it.''

Joy nodded and silently left the house, slipping out to the dark street from a side door in the courtyard. She had pulled up her veil and trailed behind Eklund and Carter as a proper Saudi Arabian woman would.

A few blocks away from the house they could see the stadium lights, which Eklund said had been left on all night last night and the night before.

Once, as they got a little closer, they were sure they heard some shooting, and farther into the city they could hear the distant wail of a siren.

Eklund led them around a corner into an alley, beyond which was a drainage ditch. The soccer stadium was across a long parking lot that was jammed with military vehicles. There was a lot of activity over there. And from here they could hear the definite rattle of small arms fire from time to time, along with screams.

"In here," Joy said as she and Eklund pried open the heavy steel lid covering a storm sewer. "It leads up into the stadium."

She went first, then Carter, and Eklund came last, easing the heavy cover back into place.

At the bottom it was pitch-black until Eklund flipped on a powerful flashlight.

They were in a bone-dry water collection junction from which four drainpipes, each about four feet in diameter, branched off.

"The big American construction company that rebuilt most of this area of downtown Riyadh convinced the Saudis they needed big storm sewers . . . in case they ever had a torrential rain," Joy said, laughing. "They're here, and no one talks about them . . . they're too embarrassed."

She ducked into one of the drainpipes, half crawling and half duck walking into the darkness. Eklund once again brought up the rear, shining the flashlight beyond them so that they could see where they were going.

The pipeline had never had water in it. The original cement dust and other debris from construction still lay everywhere.

They had gone several hundred yards, and Carter suspected they would have to be beneath the stadium by now, when Joy stopped and called for Eklund to switch off the light.

In the darkness they all held their breath, listening, and soon Carter could hear the screaming, echoing from somewhere far ahead. And he realized that he was seeing Joy's silhouette in front of him. A very dim light came from the end of the tunnel.

Silently she moved out, Carter and Eklund right on her heels, until about twenty-five yards later they came to another water collection junction. Steel rungs embedded in the concrete walls led up to a wide grating of steel bars. The light shone from above.

"Where is this?" Carter asked Joy.

"The tunnel beneath the bleachers."

"How will we know where to find the other two—Brent and Laila?"

"By now Laila has bribed one of the guards to leave a message in the bathroom just down the tunnel from here. He thinks he's doing it to get word to one of the other prisoners."

Eklund had climbed up to the grating, and he pushed two of the thick steel bars aside, making an opening large enough for them to crawl through. He disappeared over the top.

Carter and Joy scrambled up the ladder and into the wide tunnel that followed the curve of the stadium. Every fourth caged light on the rough concrete ceiling was lit. Here they could clearly hear the noise above.

"Wait here," Joy said, and she rushed down the tunnel and ducked into the bathrooms.

Eklund pulled off his headdress and the flowing robe, and tossed them down into the storm sewer. He was dressed in Saudi Army battle dress, an American M-2 carbine strapped to his back. He undid it, loaded it, and then pulled a fatigue cap out of his back pocket and pulled it low over his eyes. Carter hadn't noticed earlier, but Eklund's complexion was dark and weathered, either naturally or through makeup. But he definitely looked like an Arab now.

Carter helped him slide the heavy bars back into place so that the grating looked untouched, and a moment later Joy came out of the bathrooms.

"They're in S-seven," she said. "That's halfway around the stadium from here, up on the third level."

"We're going up there as prisoners?" Carter asked.

"That's right," Joy said. "Unless you've a better idea."

"I do," Carter said. "If the operation goes sour, they'd have us all. I'll let you two go ahead, and I'll look around on my own."

"And what the hell do you think you'll find?" Joy snapped.

"Just go up and get your friends and whoever they snagged. I'll create a diversion across the stadium from you, and I'll meet you back in the storm sewer. I'll give you ten minutes," Carter said, looking at his watch. "Then all hell will break loose." He turned on his heel and headed down the tunnel before Joy could protest.

"Damnit," he could hear Joy swear, but then he was around the curve, and when he looked back he could no longer see them.

The storm sewer had come up beneath the M section, and as Carter cautiously worked his way down the long circular tunnel, he passed markers indicating the L, K, and then J sections, each with stairways leading up. At each stairwell he stopped and listened before crossing the opening. Each time he could hear what sounded like a commotion above in the stadium proper, but until he came to the section marked I, the tunnel was deserted.

The lights were all out in this area, and he practically stumbled over the body of a nude woman lying in the middle of the floor, a large tag around the big toe on her right foot. She had been shot twice in the chest and once in the throat. It wasn't a pretty sight.

A few yards farther down the tunnel he came to several more bodies in the same condition: shot to death, tags around their big toes. Then around the curve he came to what apparently was the main morgue. Hundreds of bodies of men and women, lined up row after row, filled the tunnel.

Carter stopped in his tracks trying to make some sense of it. The Saudis thought that Israel had attacked them with nuclear weapons. Had these people been Israeli sympathizers? It was hard to tell in the dim light, but a lot of the bodies did not appear to be Arab. Carter would have bet almost anything that a good number of them were Americans or Europeans.

It was cool in the tunnel, but not *that* cool, and already a stench was beginning to accumulate. Carter had seen a lot of death before . . . too much. But this was worse than anything he could remember. These were all defenseless men and women. And for the Saudis to include the nude bodies of women down here as well, that was the ultimate insult.

He reached under his robes and pulled out his gas bomb, and then he unholstered his Luger. The storm sewer was at M, which made A or B opposite it. That meant S would be opposite F or G.

He picked his way down the long rows of bodies, his stomach churning, his anger rising. Death on this scale was absolutely senseless.

Someone said something in Arabic just down the tunnel, and Carter flattened himself against the wall. He heard someone else shout something, and then an engine started, and some kind of vehicle drove off.

For a moment or two it was silent, then two Arabs began to argue loudly, something about gold. Carter was able to catch that much; he could understand the language to some degree.

He eased a little closer, keeping flat against the wall, until he could just see the edge of a table and the hand of someone waving his arms. The voices were very loud now, and occasionally the sound of gunfire and screams came from above.

Carter slipped his thumbnail into the gas bomb's firing slot, then stepped out away from the wall.

Two Arabs, both in battle dress, their rifles leaning against the far wall, were arguing over a pallet of fully dressed bodies that had evidently just been brought down. One of them held a thick gold chain that the other obviously wanted.

"Bastards," Carter swore, and he flipped the gas bomb underhanded down the corridor and stepped back around the curve.

One of the Arabs shouted something, then Carter heard a choking sound, then nothing.

He waited a full two minutes for the gas to clear, then stepped around the corner, his Luger at the ready. Both guards were crumpled beside the pallet of bodies.

Carter grabbed one of their rifles, an American M-2 carbine, then hurried down the corridor where he pulled up short at a wide opening. A ramp led up to the open soccer arena. Here the sounds of screaming, crying, and sporadic bursts of gunfire were very loud.

He glanced at his watch. Nearly ten minutes had passed since Joy and Eklund had gone up into the stadium. They were probably still up there somewhere. He edged around the corner and started up the ramp just as a forklift, bearing another pallet of bodies, appeared at the top. He hurried back down and flicked the carbine's safety off, rounding the corner. Every muscle in his body tense, he waited.

The forklift turned the corner and was almost past him before he leaped onto the machine and hammered the rifle butt into the driver's head. The forklift slewed to the left, slamming into the wall and stalling out.

Carter jumped down and hurried back to the ramp, then raced up the hundred feet to the stadium floor, ducking down at the top so he could just see over the rail.

The stadium bleachers were well lit, as was the field. His eyes were first drawn to the huge crowd in the seats, then to the four firing squad areas on the field. As he watched, a half-dozen nude men and women were marched to the bleacher walls, while a dozen riflemen waited at ease.

He tore his eyes away from that gruesome sight and searched the bleachers directly across from where he stood.

At first he saw nothing but masses of people, but then he heard several shots, and he could see four people racing toward the exit. It was too long a distance for him to be able to pick out who it was, but he had a hunch it was Joy and Eklund and the others.

He had promised a diversion, and a diversion was what he'd give.

Everyone's attention was now on the scene at the far side of the stadium, so no one noticed when Carter jumped up and opened fire at the riflemen down on the field.

Three of them went down before bullets began ricocheting off the concrete walls where he stood, and he had to fall back.

He raced down the ramp and around the corner to where the forklift was stalled against the wall.

Using the butt of his rifle, he smashed the connectors for the LP gas tank on the back of the machine, and when it finally broke through, the gas began spurting everywhere.

Carter jumped back and hurried down the tunnel to a spot where he was just able to see the forklift and the edge of the opening to the ramp.

LP gas was forming in a boiling puddle beneath the machine when the first of the Saudi soldiers raced around the corner. Carter picked him off easily. A second and third soldier skidded around the corner, and Carter fired three shots, the first hitting the lead man, the second two slamming into the chest of the other.

He turned the carbine toward the pool of LP gas and squeezed off three quick shots, each of them ricocheting in a long line of sparks off the concrete floor.

The puddle of LP gas caught, and a second later the entire

forklift blew, flames spewing up the ramp, the concussion knocking Carter off his feet.

Men were shouting and screaming as Carter picked himself up and raced down the tunnel as fast as he could go. At each set of stairs he hesitated just long enough to fire a burst from the M-2 and, when its clip was exhausted, from his Luger.

Joy was just scrambling down the storm sewer grate when Carter came around the corner, and she almost shot him until she realized who it was.

"Come on!" she screamed. There was a lot of blood on her neck and on her right shoulder.

Eklund lay on his face on the floor.

Joy disappeared as Carter made it to the opening. No one was coming, so he pulled Eklund's body over the grate, after first checking his pulse to make sure he was dead, then climbed down the steel rungs, sliding the bars back in place.

At the bottom Joy was pulling someone into the storm sewer. She and Carter looked at each other, and then she looked up at Eklund lying on the grate.

"No . . ." she started to say, when suddenly Eklund's body was pulled aside and someone was shooting at it, the body jerking with each hit.

Carter shoved Joy farther back into the storm sewer and crawled in himself.

There was some more shooting from above, and then a silence descended over the dark tunnel.

Carter started to crawl out of the sewer pipe back into the collection junction when someone grunted behind him.

He scrambled around. "Joy?"

In the dim light from above, Carter was just able to make out Joy's figure astride the body of a man. She had a knife in her hand, and she held it very close to the man's eye.

Carter crawled back to her. The man was an Arab, and he

was frightened out of his wits. He was also wounded, blood leaking from a large hole in his chest.

"What the hell happened up there?"

Joy looked up. She was on the verge of collapse. "Brent's dead upstairs. Laila had this one cornered."

"Who is he?" Carter asked. He pulled out his penlight and shined it on the man's face, which was almost gray with fear.

"Edri el Kebir." Joy spat the name. "One of Kaddafi's terrorist lieutenants. We've been wanting to get our hands on him for a long time."

Carter had heard of him. He was an assassin. He had murdered a great number of people.

"And now, you bastard," Joy hissed, turning back to the man, and before Carter could do a thing to stop her, she flicked the tip of the knife into his left eye, completely gouging it out.

Kebir started to scream, but she clamped her left hand over his mouth and nose. He tried to struggle, but she held him tight.

"Who dropped the bombs on the oil fields?" she snapped. "Your other eye goes if you don't answer." She was speaking in French.

"*Non . . . non!*" Kebir cried when she pulled her hand away.

She made to gouge his other eye with the knife.

"Zero-hour Strike Force . . . Zero-hour Strike Force! I swear to Allah, I . . ."

"What is that?" Joy demanded.

Someone shouted from above. Kebir's remaining eye nearly bulged out of its socket, and he bit through his tongue, blood spurting everywhere.

Joy scrambled back away from him as he choked and sputtered. He'd either choke to death on his own blood or bleed to death within the next few seconds. Either way there was nothing they could do for him.

Someone above shouted again, and a burst of machine gun fire ricocheted around the collection junction.

Carter shoved past Kebir, whose struggles were rapidly weakening, and he and Joy scrambled down the tunnel as fast as they could go. There was more gunfire behind them.

Zero-hour Strike Force. What the hell was that supposed to mean? Carter asked himself. Kebir seemed to know who had made the strike. But what the hell was he talking about?

FOUR

Sirens were wailing at the soccer stadium when Carter shoved open the heavy steel cover over the storm sewer and looked outside. The air was cool, and to the east he could see that the sky was just beginning to get light. They did not have a lot of time left to get the hell away.

Across the parking lot there was a lot of activity around the stadium. Jeeps and trucks raced away, and hundreds of soldiers swarmed everywhere.

He climbed the rest of the way out of the sewer and helped Joy up, then he shoved the steel cover back into position.

Joy's veil had dropped, and he helped her fasten it in place, and then they hurried around the corner and started down the street.

The Sheraton Riyadh was at least twenty blocks away, and it would be well guarded because of the American delegation.

A jeep raced by, passing Carter and Joy who walked sedately down the street, a Saudi couple on an early-morning errand. But he sensed she was trembling.

"Laila never had a chance," she whispered harshly. Her voice had a faintly hysterical edge to it.

"Hold yourself together. We've got to make it back to

your place," Carter said. The street was clear again, and he
saw no more vehicles approaching. "Can you make it?" he
asked. It would never do for him to hold her in public, or even
for her to walk at his side. In her Arab costume she would
have to make it on her own, behind him. He just hoped that no
one would look too closely at them.

She nodded, and Carter continued down the street, aware
that she was a few paces behind him.

The sky was definitely getting lighter to the east when they
hurried across the first main intersection. Behind them military vehicles raced away from the soccer stadium in an ever
expanding search pattern. It would not be long before they
would be coming this way.

In the next block Carter ducked down a side street and a
few yards later into a narrow winding alley. A military truck
raced by, and seconds later two others passed.

"I know this alley," Joy said, catching up with him. "It
leads past the bazaar."

"Can we get to your place from here?"

"We're two blocks south, and this runs east and west."

"Can we get across?"

"I don't know."

A truck screeched to a halt out on the street, and a dozen
troops jumped down. Mindless now of how they would
appear, Carter grabbed Joy's arm and propelled her down the
alley, ducking into an open courtyard fifty yards from the
street.

They hid behind a low stone wall, and Carter pulled out his
stiletto as he held his breath, listening for the sounds of boots
on the cobblestones. If he used Wilhelmina, it would attract
the attention of the other soldiers.

Behind them was an old, ramshackle stone building, its
roof caved in, and beyond that was another stone wall, on the
other side of which was probably the street.

"Take off your robes and go back to your hotel," Joy whispered. "They're not looking for a European."

He was about to tell her not to talk, when it struck him. "What have you got on under your robes?"

"Nothing much . . . a skirt and blouse." She ripped off her veil and headdress, tossed them aside, then tried to pull off her robes but could not. She had been wounded in the shoulder and was unable to raise her right arm high enough to do it.

Someone shouted orders out in the alley, and the sound of several pairs of boots moved closer.

Carter shoved Joy farther back against the wall, then turned toward the opening and got ready to spring.

"In there," a voice said.

Carter tensed.

A soldier came into the courtyard and went immediately across to the broken-down stone building without ever turning around. He ducked inside, and Carter, keeping low, hurried after him.

It was getting very light now, and Carter looked over his shoulder toward the alley as two soldiers passed by the opening in the courtyard wall.

Immediately he ducked inside the building, coming face-to-face with the startled young soldier.

"Damn," Carter swore. He shifted the stiletto to his left hand, bunched up his right fist, and in one smooth motion clipped the young man on the jaw with every ounce of strength he had.

The soldier went down like a felled ox, his head bouncing on the dirt floor.

Hurriedly Carter stripped the soldier of his belt and boot-laces, and before he came around, he tied the young man's arms and legs. He pulled off his own headdress and used it as a gag. They'd find the soldier sooner or later.

Carter checked outside, toward the alley, but he could see no other soldiers. He hurried back to where Joy was huddled and helped her pull off her black *abaya*. Carter took off his robe and tossed it aside too, then he strapped his Luger to his left leg, beneath his trousers.

There was a long, angry red crease across Joy's shoulder, just below her neck. It had bled a lot down her side and down the front of her white blouse, but the bleeding had apparently stopped as the wound had puckered.

Carter took off his jacket and helped her put it on. It would look a little strange, but as long as she held it tightly around her neck, no one would notice she had been wounded; people would just think she was feeling the morning chill.

He sheathed his stiletto, then helped her to her feet. They hurried across the courtyard, past the broken-down building, and out the gate on the far side.

An army jeep was stationed at the end of the block to the right. Carter and Joy turned left, crossed the street, and hurried across a parking lot into a narrow winding street of tiny shops and stalls.

"This is part of the bazaar," Joy said. "We're close." She led him through the maze of tiny businesses until they finally emerged onto a back street that led into an alley behind the safe house.

Five minutes later they were inside, the doors locked, and Joy collapsed in his arms.

He picked her up and carried her into one of the main back bedrooms, and then into a large, tiled bathroom. He propped her up in a chair as he ran water in the big, sunken tub, and then he rummaged through a cabinet and found some alcohol, cotton swabs, and gauze bandages.

"Have to call the embassy," she mumbled, looking up at him as he laid the things next to her.

At first she tried to fight him as he gently took his jacket from her shoulders. But then she just slumped back as he unbuttoned her blouse and pulled it off.

There was blood everywhere from the wound, which made it look a lot worse than it actually was. He soaked the cotton swabs in alcohol and gently began cleaning the area around the wound, and then the wound itself.

She practically flew off the chair with the first touch, but then she fell back in a faint, and he quickly finished cleaning the long gash.

He removed her remaining clothes and gently lifted her into the warm water, where he washed the blood from her, then rinsed her off.

She was still unconscious when he lifted her out of the tub, dried her off, and bandaged the wound.

"What's happening . . ." she protested, coming to and stiffening in his arms as he carried her back into the bedroom.

"You're going to bed. Keep still."

He pulled the blankets back and laid her in the bed, then covered her up. For a moment or two she looked up at him with unfocused eyes, but then she fell asleep.

He brushed the long blond hair away from her eyes with his fingers. She was a very good-looking woman. She had a lovely round face, a small nose, wide dark eyes, a sensuous mouth, and a lithe body. He found himself wishing that they had met under somewhat different circumstances.

She mumbled something, but then Carter left the bedroom and went back into the rear room that they had evidently used as their operations center.

The room was furnished with a desk, a large table, and several chairs. A number of maps were tacked on one wall. An open cabinet in one corner held several bottles, some glasses, and a few mixes. Carter poured himself a brandy, neat, tossed it down, then poured himself another which he took over to the phone on the desk.

He dialed for the operator and in French asked for the Sheraton. A moment later a phone was ringing.

"*Salaam alaykum*—peace upon you. This is the Sheraton Riyadh. May we be of service?" a well-modulated man's voice asked.

"Robert Sutherland, please. He is with the American delegation."

"One moment, sir." After several seconds the telephone rang.

"Bob Sutherland here."

"How secure is this phone, Bob?" Carter asked.

Sutherland recognized his voice. "Not very. Call me in five minutes at 364.461."

Carter repeated the number and hung up. The number was probably Assistant Secretary Huntington's. There would have to be at least one secure line for him, otherwise the negotiations would be extremely difficult. Any call to Israel, or back to the President, would be unthinkable. Huntington's phone no doubt had been equipped with a scanner that would be able to detect the presence of a wiretap.

After exactly five minutes, Carter dialed the number. Sutherland answered on the first ring.

"Where the hell are you? And did you have anything to do with the trouble at the stadium?"

"I'll explain it all later. I have to get to the embassy or the hotel, and I've got a wounded girl with me."

"Saudi?"

"American. CIA."

"Goddamnit, they've probably got her on their list. They hit us with that as soon as we got off the plane. Our embassy has been surrounded. No one gets in or out, and they do mean business."

"What's the situation at the hotel?"

"They're clearing everyone out this morning. We and the

Saudi government delegation will have the entire place to ourselves, except of course for the staff, within a couple of hours.''

"We can't stay here," Carter said, trying to think it out.

"I don't know how you'll get in . . ."

"We'll be there in one hour, two at the most. I want Huntington on tap, and perhaps Hermande as well as you. If they put up a fuss, tell them to call the President for confirmation.''

"How are you getting here?" Sutherland asked after a slight hesitation.

"I'm just going to drive right up and walk right in."

"There are guards outside."

"Good," Carter said. "Just be waiting for us in the lobby. Once we get that far, we're probably going to need some help."

"You got it," Sutherland said, and Carter hung up.

He sat back with his drink and sipped it thoughtfully. What he was going to do was risky. But then, he thought, so was nuclear war.

"Aren't you going to pour me a drink?"

Carter turned around. Joy stood in the doorway. She had thrown on a bathrobe. "I thought you were sleeping."

"I'm a light sleeper whenever there's trouble. And I'm an especially light sleeper whenever a man undresses me and puts me to bed. Thanks." She had a nice smile.

Carter got up and helped her to a chair. "You lost a bit of blood. How do you feel?"

She looked up at him, her eyes wide. "Incredibly stupid that Laila, Brent, and Carl had to die."

"It couldn't be helped," Carter said. He went across the room, poured her a stiff cognac, and brought it back.

He lit a cigarette and offered it to her. She took it. He lit another for himself.

"Your diversion worked," she said after a minute. "I would never have gotten out of there without it. I didn't mean to be so hostile when we met. But you just barged in on our operation . . ."

Carter said nothing as he watched her. Her hard edge of professionalism was beginning to slip.

"Who are you?" she suddenly asked. "I know everyone over at State. You don't work for Harry Hall."

"No, I don't," Carter said.

"Who then?"

He hesitated. "Are you up to getting dressed?"

Her nostrils flared. But she nodded.

"Have you got a car?"

"Around the side, in the garage. It's an old Ford, but it runs."

"Go get dressed. We're leaving here within the hour . . . unless you want to stay."

"I should return to the embassy."

Carter explained what Sutherland had told him and what he proposed to do.

"Doesn't leave me much choice, does it?" she said, getting painfully to her feet.

He jumped up to help her. But she brushed his hand aside. "Once is enough," she said. "When I'm undressed in front of a man, I'd prefer to be in shape to enjoy it."

She left the room, and Carter finished his drink, stubbed out his cigarette, and went in search of the old Ford that still ran.

The garage was at the side of the courtyard and opened directly onto a narrow street. A truck rumbled by outside, and through a crack in the door Carter watched it until it disappeared around the corner at the end of the block. He went in the little wooden building and looked at the car. It was a very old Thunderbird, probably a '62 or '63, and was incredibly beat up. The desert sun and sand had scoured every bit of paint from the body, making it look almost like a hand-hammered aluminum model of a car, done by an exceedingly poor craftsman.

The interior of the car was all torn up, and where the radio had been, there was a large, gaping hole, wires hanging loose.

A key was in the ignition. He slipped behind the wheel, pumped the gas a couple of times, and turned the key. The car started immediately, the engine ticking over smoothly and quietly.

He shut it off, got out, and had started back to the house, when he saw Joy come through the courtyard. The change in her appearance was nothing less than startling. She had fixed her hair and had put on some makeup. She wore a light-colored summer dress and sandals, and carried a pretty straw hat and matching bag. She had thrown a shawl over her shoulders to cover the bandages. She looked very chic and French, certainly nothing like an undercover intelligence service operative who a short while ago had been torturing a man for information.

"Surprised?" she asked, delighted with his reaction.

"How do you feel?" he asked.

"I'm on my feet, but I wouldn't want to run the fifty-yard dash."

He took her arm, and they went back into the garage, where he helped her into the car. He went around to the driver's side, started the engine, then jumped out and looked outside. When he was sure there was no traffic, he leaped back in the car and squealed out of the garage and down the street.

At the corner he turned right, then left, finally coming back to Ras Hanna.

There were a lot of military vehicles and a few civilian

trucks. Joy directed Carter in the opposite direction from the soccer stadium to the downtown area where the hotel was located.

Sandbagged machine gun emplacements and trucks with antiaircraft rocket launchers seemed to be stationed in every empty parking lot and open field.

Downtown, cops were directing the increasing early morning traffic, and no one gave the ancient Ford a second glance until they came to within a block of the Sheraton, which was an ultramodern glass and steel structure. There were a lot of military vehicles as well as soldiers on foot throughout the area.

At the avenue that led to the hotel, they were waved to the left, and Carter dutifully turned, pulling up and parking half a block away.

The hotel was in the middle of the block and faced a line of office buildings and a department store.

Carter buttoned his jacket as he got out of the car, went around to help Joy out, and together they continued down the block to the service alley that ran behind the buildings across the street from the hotel.

No one paid them any attention as they ducked down the alley and finally mounted the service platform at the rear of the department store.

Joy realized what he was trying to do, and he could see that she was trying desperately to hold herself together although she was in some pain. There was a small amount of blood on her shawl; her wound had begun to leak.

The rear door was open, and they went inside to the shipping and receiving area. No one was around. Across the room, they went through the swinging doors into a wide corridor, off which several offices opened. At the end of the corridor was the large billing and posting office, and still no one paid them much attention as they crossed the big room that contained at least a dozen men in Arab robes busy at their desks.

On the far side of the room they emerged into another corridor that finally led into the main floor of the store itself.

There was no one in the store. The overhead lights were out, and many of the displays were covered with white drop cloths.

Carter looked at his watch. It was well after seven o'clock. The store was due to open at eight, and there were office workers in the back. But where were the sales clerks?

He and Joy crossed the main floor, threading their way through the counters and displays to the front glass doors.

Military jeeps with .50-caliber machine guns mounted on the backs were stationed just outside the hotel across the street. There were soldiers everywhere, manning the sandbagged gun emplacements. The place looked as if it were under siege, which in a way it was. The entire country was.

The department store had apparently been closed for regular business because of the proximity of the American delegation.

"What are we going to do?" Joy asked.

Carter stared across at the hotel entrance. It was not more than a hundred feet away.

He looked back at the department store counters filled with goods. And suddenly he had it.

"Stay here," he said, and he turned and hurried back into the store, to the women's section that was filled with veils and silk things.

He quickly gathered great armloads of designer negligees and peignoirs, then at the perfume counter he grabbed several large bottles, then went back to the front doors where Joy was waiting wide-eyed for him.

"Ready?" Carter asked brightly. "You're the French

fashion consultant for the store, and I'm your man Friday. This stuff has been ordered by Mr. Huntington himself. Mr. Sutherland will be waiting for us in the lobby.''

She looked back out at the street. "It's so crazy, it just might work," she said, grinning. She looked back. "*Allons*," she said. "Let's go!''

"*Oui, mademoiselle!*''

Carter reached inside his coat for his Luger, made sure the safety was off, and made sure it was totally concealed beneath the silky lingerie he was holding. Joy unlocked the front doors and they stepped outside.

"Don't take no for an answer," Carter whispered urgently as they stepped across the sidewalk and off the curb.

Immediately a half-dozen soldiers sat up, and before Carter and Joy got halfway to the hotel, an officer rushed up to them.

"What is this?" he shouted in Arabic. "Go back! Go back!''

Joy gave him her most outraged look. "What do you mean?" she asked in French. "We are bringing only what Monsieur Huntington has asked us to bring. Step aside and let us pass.''

Carter had the concealed Luger pointed at the confused officer.

"Let us through, please. Monsieur Sutherland is waiting for us in the lobby," Joy said imperiously. "Who is your superior officer?''

"Come," the officer said. "We will see.''

He escorted them the rest of the way across the street and into the hotel. Sutherland was waiting there by the front desk.

"Ah, Monsieur Sutherland," Carter cried out, rushing to him. "Tell this man that we are here to see Monsieur Huntington.''

Sutherland's eyes were bulging out of their sockets as he

took in Carter, half-buried under a mountain of lingerie and perfume, and the attractive blonde at his side. He swallowed, then nodded at the officer. ''That's right . . . that's right— Secretary Huntington asked them here.''

The officer looked doubtfully from Sutherland to Carter and Joy, and then back again. Finally he nodded. ''You will be responsible for them, sir,'' he said. Then he turned on his heel and marched out the door.

''This way,'' Sutherland said, and he led them back across the lobby to the elevators. There were several people standing around, and they were all staring.

Once the elevator doors closed and they started up, Sutherland breathed a deep sigh of relief. ''Jesus Christ, I didn't have the faintest idea what you were trying to pull.''

''Just get us to Huntington . . .'' Carter started to say, when Joy's knees buckled beneath her and she collapsed against a wall.

Carter dropped everything and grabbed her before she hit the floor.

FIVE

Roger Sellkirk, one of the special presidential appointees on the mission, was actually Dr. Sellkirk. By the time Carter left Joy, she was resting comfortably.

"She's lost a lot of blood, and it looks as if she's been under a great deal of strain lately," the tall, lanky doctor said.

"But she'll be all right?" Carter asked.

"Absolutely. She just needs a little rest. I gave her something to make her sleep, something for the pain, and a course of antibiotics. She'll be fine."

"Thanks," Carter said, and he went with Sutherland out of the doctor's suite and down the corridor to the master suite which Huntington and Hermande had designated as their operational headquarters.

There was a great deal of activity out in the corridor. The American delegation had taken over the top floor, the Saudis the next floor down, and the Swiss Red Cross the floor below that.

No journalists were allowed within a half mile of the hotel.

Before they went in, Sutherland took Carter aside. "I think I'd better tell you that Huntington is mad as hell about this."

Carter said nothing.

"He's convinced you're doing your damnedest to screw

up his best efforts at these peace talks. This is his show. He'll fight anything that takes it out of his hands."

Carter nodded. "Thanks for the tip, Bob."

"Just watch yourself. He's a powerful man just at this moment."

They walked the rest of the way to the master suite in silence. Sutherland knocked once, and they went in. There was an ornately furnished sitting room, two bedrooms, each with its own bathroom, and a tiny kitchenette.

Huntington was on the phone when they came in. He looked up, said something that Carter couldn't quite catch, then hung up. There was no one else in the suite.

"Secretary Huntington, you may remember Mr. Carter," Sutherland said as they approached.

Carter held out his hand, but Huntington ignored it.

"I have been on the phone with the secretary of state, the secretary of defense, the Joint Chiefs, and just minutes ago, with the Vice-President. And I can tell you that no one likes what is happening here. You were sent here to aid our best efforts. So far, from what I can see, you have set about doing exactly the opposite. Can you explain that, Mr. Carter?"

"I think I can," Carter said.

"Were you involved in the disturbance at the soccer stadium?" Huntington asked. He was angry, and he seemed about ready to explode.

"I caused it . . . or at least I was a part of the cause."

Huntington just looked at him.

Quickly Carter explained exactly what had happened from the moment the last of the crew left Air Force One until he and Joy showed up here, including the events at the stadium and the Libyan terrorist's admission of the words "Zero-hour Strike Force."

For several seconds Huntington just looked at Carter. But

then he shook his head in exasperation. "Are you trying to tell me that you suspect the Libyans of dropping the bombs on the Saudi oil fields?"

"I'm telling you that a Libyan terrorist knew about it. And I do not think the Israelis were behind this."

Huntington turned away a moment. "The Central Intelligence Agency had no business operating here, in a friendly country. No business whatsoever."

Carter couldn't believe what he was hearing. "If the CIA had not been working here, we'd never have found out about the Libyan connection."

"It's hard to believe such a story! Execution squads? Rows of naked bodies at the soccer stadium? This is crazy!"

The door burst open and one of Huntington's aides rushed in. "They've taken over the hotel! The Swiss and the Saudis below us have all gone. The soldiers . . . they're downstairs right now . . ."

Carter and Sutherland raced to the windows at the same moment. Below, on the street, there were three tanks, and the entire block was swarming with soldiers and civilians. The hotel was definitely under attack.

"Why?" Huntington said.

"Try the phone," Carter snapped, and Sutherland hurried across the room.

"The phone is dead," Sutherland said.

"Get everyone in here on the double. It won't take long for the Saudis to get upstairs. When they do, Huntington is to demand to speak to our President and to demand an explanation for what's happening."

"What about you?"

"No one has ever heard of me," Carter said. "You're going to have to somehow stall them on Joy's identity. If they find out she's CIA, they'll probably kill her. Tell her I'm following up the Kebir lead.''

"But how are you going to get out of here?'' Sutherland asked as Carter headed out the door.

"With the Swiss delegation.''

"But they're gone!''

"I know,'' Carter said. He raced down the corridor to the stairwell, threw open the door, and hesitated for just a moment on the landing, listening. There was a great deal of activity below. But it definitely sounded as if it was down on the ground floor. They were starting up.

Taking the stairs two and three at a time, Carter raced down two flights, reaching the floor the Swiss Red Cross delegation had occupied just as the Saudi soldiers were coming up.

The corridor was deserted as Carter raced away from the stairwell and around the corner toward the elevators. He pulled out his stiletto, quickly picked the lock of a room just across from the elevators, and let himself in.

The beds had not been made nor had the bathroom been cleaned. At the windows he looked down into the rear parking lot. It was crammed with soldiers and a shouting mob of civilians. Four tanks had been pulled up, their guns covering the back of the hotel.

He turned and looked back toward the door. There was only one way he was going to get out of here. It would be a long shot.

He went back to the door and opened it. Then he mussed up his hair, pulled his tie half off, unbuttoned the top two buttons of his shirt, pulled out his shirttail, and pulled off one shoe. He staggered like that to the elevator, and pushed the button. Then he banged on the elevator door.

"*Was ist los?*'' he shouted in German. He punched the elevator button again, and the car that had been on the first floor started up. He banged on the door harder. *"Was gibt? Was ist los?"*

When the elevator doors opened, Carter stumbled backward as if he were half drunk. Four soldiers and an officer stepped out into the corridor.

"Was wollen Sie?" Carter demanded. "Where are my friends? What is happening here?"

"You are Swiss?" the officer asked in German.

"Of course I am Swiss, you idiot!" Carter shouted. "I am Red Cross," he said and reached inside his jacket as if going for his identification, but his fingers curled around the butt of his Luger.

The officer shook his head in disgust. "Your colleagues are already gone. They left an hour ago. They are at the airport by now."

"But . . . what am I to do?" Carter said, bewildered.

The officer made some rude remark in Arabic to his men, and then he detailed two of them to escort the drunken Swiss. "They will take you to your people at the airport. We will radio ahead. Do not worry. We want you out of our country as badly as you want to leave."

Carter staggered, and the officer looked past him through the open door of the room.

"What about your luggage? Are you going to leave it here?"

Carter looked back toward the room. "It is gone. They took it. I don't even have a clean shirt."

The officer shook his head again. "Get him out of here. I'll call the airport commander."

Carter let himself be escorted onto the elevator, downstairs, and across the lobby. There were soldiers everywhere, but no one paid them much attention.

His escorts dumped him in the back seat of a jeep, and they

headed away from the hotel at high speed. He looked back, and it gave him an odd feeling to realize that Huntington and the others, plus the Americans at the embassy across town, were being held hostage. At any moment, whatever force had attacked the oil fields could decide to drop a nuclear device on this city. The death toll would be terrible. *U.S. forces will have to intervene*, Carter thought. *We can't allow the takeover of oil resources that we depend upon.* But the Soviets probably had the same ideas in mind, and they might also have thought it time to intervene here.

He shuddered to think what was possibly beginning and just how fragile world peace really was at this moment.

They made it to the airport in less than twenty minutes, where the jeep was admitted through a side gate, and they drove around to the flightline side of the terminal. Air Force One was still parked beneath the tarp in front of the main terminal entrance, but on the far side of the parking apron, about a half mile away, was a 707 with the red-and-white Swiss flag on the tail and the International Red Cross symbol on the body.

There was a knot of people at the boarding stairs. The plane was obviously ready for takeoff, and they were waiting for him.

The jeep pulled up, and before his escorts could help him, Carter hopped out, hurried to one of the Swiss delegates, and half fell on him.

"They think I'm Swiss! I'm an American journalist! Help me!" Carter whispered urgently in German.

At first it didn't seem as if the Swiss understood what it was Carter wanted. But then the soldiers came up and saluted.

"Is this man one of yours?"

Come on, Carter prayed.

"Yes, he is one of ours," the Swiss said, looked at Carter disgustedly. "Where did you find him?"

"He was still at the hotel. Drunk!"

"I am terribly sorry about this," the Swiss said, and a couple of others took Carter and helped him up the boarding stairs. He could barely suppress a grin.

"We will leave now, if we have our clearance, although I must vigorously protest the treatment we have—"

"We are at war, sir," one of the soldiers said.

"With whom?" the Swiss delegate snapped.

The soldiers turned on their heels, got back into the jeep, and drove away.

For a moment or two the Swiss delegation watched the jeep round the corner, and then they turned and came up the stairs and into the plane.

Carter had been led to one of the rear seats.

"Just who the hell are you?" one of his escorts asked in German.

"Nick Carter. I'm a journalist with Amalgamated Press and Wire Services out of Washington, D.C."

The hatch was shut, and a second later the engines were started and the cabin was pressurized. The delegate who had vouched for Carter came back. He seemed angry.

"Now just who are you and what is this all about?"

Carter explained his wire service cover.

"How did you get into the hotel?"

"With the American delegation, sir," Carter said. "And I want to thank you for helping me."

"But I don't understand, Mr. Carter. If you were there obviously covering the biggest exclusive in years, why did you want so desperately to get out of Saudi Arabia?"

"As soon as your delegation left, the hotel was seized by the military. Our embassy has also been seized."

"My God," the delegate breathed. "Another Tehran hostage situation?"

"I'm afraid so, sir. I just barely managed to escape."

They were at the end of the runway, and everyone sat down and strapped in for the takeoff roll. As soon as they were airborne, the delegate got up and started forward, but Carter called after him.

"Are we going to Bern or Geneva?"

The man looked back. "Neither. We're going to Cairo. We're going to set up shop there."

It was noon, and the hot desert sun blazed in the Egyptian sky as the Swiss Red Cross plane landed in Cairo. Carter was passed through Egyptian customs with the Swiss delegates without being searched. He merely showed his American passport, which elicited not the slightest interest, and then they were outside waiting for taxis.

"Good luck to you, Mr. Carter," the delegate who had vouched for him said. They shook hands.

"Good luck to us all," Carter said.

It took more than an hour for Carter to get a cab and make it through Cairo's almost impassible traffic to the American embassy. He showed his passport at the front desk to a harried clerk.

"I need to see the ambassador."

"He's not in Cairo at the moment, sir."

"Then the chargé d'affaires."

The clerk raised his eyebrows. "What may I ask is the nature of your problem?"

"I just escaped from the Sheraton Riyadh, where the American delegation, led by Assistant Secretary of State Howard Huntington, is being held hostage."

"Good God," the clerk breathed. He came around the counter. "Please come this way, sir," he said.

Carter followed him to the end of the corridor, then up to the third floor where he was shown into an office with a view of the city.

A moment later a middle-aged man with graying hair came in, closing the door behind him. "Now, what's this story I hear . . ."

Carter had been standing by the window. "Sorry to bother you like this, sir, but I'll need the use of your Stateside communications facility for a top-secret transmission. Immediately."

The chargé d'affaires just stood there for a moment. "There is no such facility here."

"You'll have either a KO-6, which is your voice-encrypted facility, or perhaps a KW-26, which is teletype. Either way they'll be routed through Ramstein Air Force Base in Germany, and from there to the Pentagon for distribution."

"I think I'd better see your passport, sir."

"I'll give you the routing codes," Carter said. "You can set up the circuit and verify my access first." He grabbed pen and paper from the desk and quickly wrote out the codes that would connect him with David Hawk at AXE, day or night.

He handed it to the chargé. "I'd prefer the voice circuit."

The man looked at the slip of paper, then turned and left the room.

Carter turned back to the window and lit a cigarette. During the entire eleven-hundred-mile flight, the Swiss had talked nonstop about the situation at the hotel. Carter told them about the goings-on at the soccer stadium, and none of them seemed surprised. An Israeli activist had claimed responsibility for the nuclear strike. And anyone with the slightest hint of Israeli sympathies had been arrested.

"But that had been going on for at least two days," Carter protested.

"The aircraft that delivered the bombs had Israeli markings. There were witnesses twenty miles away who saw the planes flying very low over the desert afterward."

"We will try to do something about it, Mr. Carter," one of the other delegates had said. "But we cannot promise much."

Carter was tired now. And he thought about Joy Makepiece. If it was within Sutherland's power to protect her, Carter knew the man would do his best. Yet he had hated leaving her like that.

The chargé came back with a highly deferential attitude. "Sorry to have kept you waiting, sir. Your circuit is ready." He came around behind the desk, opened a drawer, and lifted out a plain black telephone with a red button. He picked up the receiver, punched the button, and then handed it to Carter.

"I will be just outside if you need anything, sir."

"Thanks," Carter said. He waited until the man was gone, then picked up the phone. "Carter here."

"How did you get to Cairo, and have you come up with anything yet, N3?" Hawk said, his voice gruff. It was very early in the morning in Washington.

Quickly Carter explained about Joy and the other CIA operatives working out of the safe house, the incident at the soccer stadium, and finally their entry to, and his exit from, the hotel.

"Zero-hour Strike Force," Hawk said. "Hold on and I'll have Smitty see what Archives can come up with." He was off the line for just a moment. "What's your next move?"

"I'm going to Tripoli, sir," Carter said. "Ms. Makepiece identified this Edri el Kebir as one of Kaddafi's lieutenants. It's not much of a lead, but it's something."

"Use your French passport. Claude Avorix runs an import-export business there. He's a friend."

"French Secret Service?"

"Yes, SDECE," Hawk said. "Smitty's on. What'd you find?"

"Nothing, and yet something, sir," Smitty said over the encrypted line. "The term 'Zero-hour Strike Force' has apparently been flagged in our reference section."

"But?" Hawk prompted.

"The computer files have been erased."

SIX

The chargé d'affaires, F. Monkton Clarke, turned out to be a bright, very capable man, and by four in the afternoon, Carter was being piloted in a twin-engine Beechcraft up the coast toward the Libyan border nearly four hundred miles distant.

His pilot was Ben Sidirin, a former Egyptian fighter pilot who now worked for the American embassy. For the most part his job consisted of flying VIP guests around Cairo, up to Alexandria, around the Pyramids, and up and down a hundred miles or so of the Nile.

During the two-hour flight to the tiny coastal fishing town of Salûm, which was just across the border from its sister town El Bardi in Libya, Sidirin talked nonstop about his relatives. It seems he had dozens of them who worked for numerous governmental agencies in Cairo.

It suddenly occurred to Carter that Sidirin was spying on the American embassy for his own government. But he was so obvious it was almost laughable. Clarke had to know about the man, but this flight really didn't matter. Egypt and Libya were not on the best of terms. It wouldn't benefit the Egyptian government to let Kaddafi know that an American had been allowed to sneak into his country.

In fact, he thought, if Clarke and the embassy staff were on the ball, they'd have fed Sidirin whatever information they wanted the Egyptians to have, and held back on the rest. A spy such as this, out in the open and in plain sight of everyone, was certainly preferable to a deep-cover man, even if the deep agent was suspect.

"Have you any relatives in Salûm?" Carter asked the little pilot.

"Yes! Yes, of course," the man said. "I have a second cousin on the fisheries board. He also runs a fleet of fishing boats. Alas, they are doing so poorly now, they lately have taken to smuggling. Cigarettes and whiskey, don't you know, up to Tobruk."

"What is this cousin's name?"

Sidirin laughed. "His name? We are friends, Mr. Carter. Are you interested in the fisheries business, perhaps?"

"Let's just say I'm interested in getting to Tobruk without the stupid formalities of a border crossing. It could be very profitable for your cousin . . . and for you as well."

"American dollars? Perhaps five thousand for me, five thousand for my cousin?"

Carter smiled. He reached into his jacket pocket and pulled out one of the packets of diamonds. He opened it and handed it over to the pilot, whose eyes went wide. The plane dipped down and slewed to the left before Sidirin regained control. But he didn't spill one of the diamonds.

"They are real," Carter said. "And the manner of their division between you and your cousin I will leave entirely to you. I merely wish to be taken to Tobruk without fuss and without questions."

"It will be as you wish, Mr. Carter," Sidirin said. He looked lovingly at the diamonds again, then carefully folded the packet with one hand and stuffed it deep into an inside pocket. "Indeed," he said, smiling. "It will be as you ask."

Carter leaned over a little closer. "One thing, Ben," he said, his voice low.

Sidirin's eyes narrowed. "I wouldn't cheat you!" he stammered in alarm.

"You will be a dead man should I not reach Tobruk safely. But not by my hands. By your own government's hands for taking bribes from an American spy."

Sidirin turned white. But he said nothing for the remainder of the trip, making a beautiful landing at the government field outside the small town.

They borrowed an ancient rattletrap of a Chevy van, and Sidirin drove him into the tiny fishing village of about a thousand people.

The sun was just going down on the western horizon when they pulled up behind a collection of old, decrepit stone huts with tin roofs about a hundred yards up from a stony beach. A half-dozen heavy-looking open fishing boats rested on the beach. Anchored fifty yards out was a much larger boat, a dhow, its lateen sail furled and taken in for the night. A light breeze ruffled the water, causing the big boat to bob gently at her mooring.

"Good, they are back," Sidirin said, climbing out of the van.

Carter followed him across to one of the huts, then waited outside while the Egyptian pilot talked his "deal" with his cousin.

It took less than five minutes, and Carter was invited inside. There were four fishermen there, drinking very thick, very sweet coffee. They invited Carter to sit, and another cup was produced.

No one had poured Sidirin a cup, and after a few moments, the largest of the men got up and went outside with him. They were gone fifteen or twenty minutes during which time Carter had two more cups of the vile-tasting coffee and listened to the fishermen tell stories about their day's catch, which included him.

At length the big man came back, and Carter looked up. Sidirin wasn't with him.

"Ben is gone back Cairo. Fly back. We go in one hour."

"How long will it take to get to Tobruk?"

"All night, all day, then late at night."

He had hoped for something a lot faster, but it could not be helped now. He nodded.

"Good," the big fisherman said, slapping him on the back.

Carter never learned the names of Sidirin's cousin or his three crewmen, but at around eight o'clock, carrying their provisions with them, they rowed out to the large dhow, set sail, and traveled well out into the Mediterranean; Carter guessed at least thirty miles, perhaps more. Then they turned west with an increasingly strong northerly wind that shot them like an express train over and through all but the very largest of the waves.

He managed to get some sleep, forward under the overhang on the mostly open deck, one hand inside his jacket on his Luger in case they tried to rob him and throw him overboard. But they made no move against him.

By morning the seas had moderated somewhat, and the crew made some hot tea to go with their meal of bread and goat cheese, topped off by dates and figs.

It was pleasantly warm and peaceful on the water as the sun climbed higher into the sky at their backs. Once, sometime before noon, they saw the trails of four very high-flying jets, and twice in the afternoon they saw large ships well beyond them out to sea, racing fast to the east.

"It is the American Navy," one of the fishermen said. "They are on their way to Israel."

So close, Carter mused, *and yet so very far away*. It was peaceful out here, but now they were offshore of Kaddafi's Libya. And well out to sea were American naval war vessels. It was somehow incongruous.

The wind died completely in the early afternoon, and the four of them took turns sculling the heavy dhow through the flat, calm sea.

At about four o'clock, however, the wind came up again, and within a half hour, they were once again roaring across a sea studded with whitecaps in every direction.

There was no compass on the boat, and when the sky clouded over and night fell, Carter was certain they'd have to turn toward shore. But the big fisherman did not alter his course until nearly ten, when he finally turned toward what Carter took to be south and the Libyan shore.

The glow of Tobruk showed up on the horizon within a half hour, and by 11:30 they were picking out individual lights as well as the blinking red lights on the radio tower.

"We put you ashore west of city," Sidirin's cousin said. "There is good beach there and not so many lights."

"How far to the highway?" Carter asked.

"Not far," the big man said. "Five hundred meters. Is good?"

"Is very good," Carter said.

It was well after 2:00 A.M. by the time they stopped just offshore and a small dinghy was lowered over the side.

Carter shook hands all around. "Thank you," he said.

"You have paid well," Sidirin's cousin said, and Carter climbed down into the rowboat with one of the other men.

Five minutes later the rowboat was heading back to the dhow, and Carter stood on Libyan soil. As an American he'd be shot on sight if he were discovered. He was going to have to be very careful.

He lit a cigarette and, cupping the lit end in his hand,

trudged up from the beach over a series of dunes, walking across a wide field of low brush, then up a steep embankment and finally onto the surface of the paved highway.

Tobruk was not a very large town; it had less than twenty thousand people. But there was nothing else along the coast for a long way in either direction, so its lights ten miles away lit up the night sky. A few miles up the highway was the rotating green and white light of an airport.

Carter looked in the opposite direction down the long dark highway. It was more than six hundred air miles from here to Tripoli, and because of the way the coast curved, perhaps half again that far by highway. He had wasted too much time on the dhow. He was rested. Well fed. It was time to move fast now.

He turned and started down the highway toward the airport. One way or another, he was going to be in Tripoli before lunch.

A wide, well-paved road led from the main coastal highway back to the airport, which turned out to be a small commercial field. In this Carter felt lucky. Had there been any military stationed at the field, security would have been tight.

The small terminal building was open but deserted when Carter walked in. He went across to the door that led out onto the field and looked outside.

The taxiway and runway lights were off; only the rotating green and white light atop the terminal building gave any indication that this was a working airport. To the left were three large hangars. Attached to the side of the nearest one was what appeared to be an office. A light was shining in the window.

He stepped out of the terminal and headed down the parking apron to the office. He knocked at the door and let himself in.

An older man, who appeared to be American or European, was sitting back, his feet up on a battered wooden desk, sound asleep. He had long, dirty gray hair, wore boots and khaki trousers, and a scuffed leather jacket was thrown over his shoulders. He obviously had been drinking. The tiny office reeked of booze.

Carter took out a packet of diamonds, opened it, and laid it on the desk. Then he lit a cigarette and sat down.

The nameplate on the desk said Arbogast. Carter reached forward and shoved the man's feet off the desk.

"Monsieur Arbogast?"

The man's feet hit the floor, and he sat up sputtering. "What the bleedin' hell . . ." He realized he was not alone and reached for the desk drawer.

Carter sat forward and grabbed his wrist. He smiled. "I don't especially like Brits, you know," he said in English with a heavy French accent. "But if you will look on your desk you will see the present I have brought you."

Slowly the man's eyes left Carter's, and he looked down at the open packet of diamonds. His eyes widened, and he licked his lips.

Carter released his wrist and sat back. With shaking hands the man examined the diamonds a little more closely, finally looking up. Sweat had beaded on his upper lip.

"Who do you want me to kill, Monsieur . . ."

"My name is of no consequence. And I do not require that sort of work."

"What then? Smuggling?"

"Don't be tedious," Carter said in French, then switched to English: "My automobile is in town. Completely ruined. It is something with the motor . . . seizing or something because of the heat."

Arbogast nodded. He glanced at the stones. "You want me to take you somewhere? Crete, maybe?"

"Tripoli."

Arbogast's eyebrows came up. "You surprise me. I've not heard of you . . . of a Frenchman doing business in Tobruk."

"Nor have I heard of you. I do not need introductions. I need a pilot."

"When?"

"This morning. I wish to be in Tripoli certainly no later than noon."

Arbogast looked at his watch. "It'll be light in a few hours. We'll go then."

"Why not now?"

"The generator for the runway lights has gone bad. Besides, we've lost our clearance for night flights. We can leave in the morning as soon as it's light enough to see."

"We will be there before noon, with no interference?"

"Guaranteed," Arbogast said. "We'll have to make two stops to refuel—one at Benghazi and the second one at Misurata across the Gulf of Sidra."

Carter nodded. Arbogast folded the packet of diamonds and pocketed them.

"I have two airplanes, a very good DC-3 and a small DeHavilland. We'll take the small plane. It will attract less attention."

The DeHavilland was a very old Otter, the same kind of cargo-carrying light plane that Canadian and Alaskan bush pilots used. It was a little after 5:00 A.M. when they went out to it, and Arbogast made a brief walk-around inspection before they climbed inside and strapped in.

They had talked through the morning. Carter had learned that Ralph Arbogast had been born in Liverpool, but after some trouble with the law in London—which he did not go into—he had come here to North Africa to fly anybody or anything for a price. Here he had remained, finally ending up a few years ago in Tobruk after some trouble in Algiers.

"I have to stay away from the big cities," he explained. "Too much trouble there for the likes of me."

He called the military base east of town on the radio for flight clearance, and then they were airborne, climbing up into the brilliantly clear air, the startlingly blue Mediterranean to their right, and the faded brown desert to their left.

It was nearly seven-thirty when they landed at the sleepy Benghazi airport to refuel, which took nearly forty-five minutes. It was well after ten when they again refueled at Misurata, getting airborne at quarter to eleven.

At exactly noon they touched down at Tripoli's large airport, military aircraft parked in long rows across the field from the terminal.

A French airliner had just come in, and it was disgorging its passengers as Arbogast taxied over to the business aviation terminal.

"Will I be required to go through any customs check?" Carter asked.

"No. In fact you won't even have to go over to the main terminal. Someone here at the business terminal will take you into town if you like."

"Thanks," Carter said.

"You've made me a rich man. I should thank *you*," Arbogast said, bringing the plane to a halt but not cutting the engines.

"You're not coming in?"

He shook his head. "Big cities are trouble. Tripoli now for me, with my new sparkling pals, here," he said, patting his pocket, "would be disastrous. No, I'm going back to Tobruk where it's a damn sight safer."

They shook hands, and Carter got out of the plane and went into the business terminal, where he hired a taxi to take him into town. He was just leaving the airport area a half hour later when he looked back and saw the DeHavilland taking off.

Tripoli was alive with people and traffic, so it took the better part of an hour to make it into town and to the waterfront district. They drove past Avorix Import/Export, housed in a large warehouse on the quay, and stopped a couple of blocks later at a small hotel.

When the taxi was out of sight, Carter walked back to the warehouse and entered by a side door marked Office.

The place was a madhouse. A large French cargo vessel was being unloaded. A dozen forklifts scurried back and forth, and twenty or thirty men swarmed on and around the ship.

Carter was directed to a glassed-in suite of offices on a balcony in the back. He went up the stairs, knocked, and went inside. An attractive young woman sat behind a desk. She looked up from her typewriter. *"Monsieur?"*

"I am Marcel Mentoir. I am here to speak with Monsieur Avorix."

"He is very busy, but I will see if he can spare you a moment," the girl said. She was dark, with high cheekbones and a fine, delicate nose. She picked up the phone. "Claude, there is a Monsieur Mentoir to see you." She paused a moment, looked up in surprise, then nodded her head. *"Oui,"* she said and hung up the phone. "Please go in," she said, pointing toward a door. "He will be right up."

"Merci," Carter said with a smile, and he entered Avorix's tastefully furnished, air-conditioned office. The far wall was mostly window, and Carter looked out on the ship and down at the workmen on the docks. It was a spectacular view.

He lit a cigarette and watched what was going on below for a few minutes. Soon the door opened behind him, and a short, pudgy, balding man breezed in.

"I can see what is happening on my docks from there," he said. He came across the room and pumped Carter's hand. "I trust there was no trouble making it here?"

Carter told him about Arbogast.

"I know him. Not a bad sort, but he can't pay his gambling debts. There are a number of unsavory characters in Algiers who would like to talk to him."

Avorix poured them both a cognac, and they sat down.

"How secure is your office?" Carter began.

"Very," Avorix said. "It's swept daily. Hawk got a message to me about you. I understand you know something of the nuclear attack on the Saudis."

"Perhaps," Carter said. "But I am going to need your help. There may be a connection here, to Libya."

"With Kaddafi?"

Carter nodded.

Avorix laughed. "You Americans have become paranoid over our ludicrous colonel. But how do you think he is involved in this?"

Very briefly Carter described to Avorix what had happened at the soccer stadium in Riyadh, including Kebir's name and the Zero-hour Strike Force.

Avorix sat back in his chair, deep in thought for several moments. "Kebir in Riyadh," he said. "It could not simply be a coincidence. And yet . . ."

"And yet what?"

"Libya has no reason to attack Saudi Arabia, even if she did have nuclear weapons."

"The Saudis are friendly with the U.S."

Avorix shrugged. "There are other, more enticing targets if that is the criteria. No, it is something more than that. And then this business of the Zero-hour Strike Force. I have not heard of it before, but it sounds ominous."

"There's no possibility that Kaddafi could have gotten hold of four nuclear devices? They weren't very large."

"The Israeli planes and ground equipment, yes, easily. But the nuclear weapons? I have worked here for ten years— ten active years—and I have found no evidence that he has managed to come up with a nuclear force. He has tried. He does have the money. But no one trusts him."

"We have to find out very soon. War will erupt unless we can come up with proof that the Israelis did not do it."

"Are you so sure they didn't?"

"Yes," Carter said.

"Very well, what is it I can do to help?"

"Who did Kebir work for?"

"Kaddafi."

"I meant, who was his direct boss?"

Avorix shrugged again. "I do not know, for certain, although I have my suspicions."

"I want to get to the man, whoever he is. Immediately. Tonight if possible."

"To do what? Kill him?" Avorix asked. "You would never get out of Libya."

"To talk with him. Kebir knows of this Zero-hour Strike Force, whatever it is. And he was in Saudi Arabia. His boss should know more."

"Yes," Avorix said thoughtfully. "And then what, when you have your information. What will you do with it?"

"Act on it."

"You mean bring the proof back to Riyadh with you?"

"Possibly that."

"Or? Perhaps you discover it was Kaddafi's doing."

"I would kill him," Carter said.

"I see," Avorix said. He got up and came around the desk. "You will have to remain here. I will have Marie bring you something to eat later this afternoon. For now there is cognac and wine, and there are cigarettes. Please help yourself. I will be gone for a while . . . probably several hours."

"We have to do this tonight."

"I will have something arranged for tonight. Meanwhile, do not leave this office. There is no need to expose yourself until it is absolutely necessary."

SEVEN

Marie, Avorix's secretary, brought Carter his lunch at around 2:30, then hurried back out of the office as if she thought he might bite her. She had brought him a couple of bottles of ice cold beer, some bread, cheese, and several different kinds of sausage; all of it was very good.

Before he had gone out, the little Frenchman had shown Carter where the shortwave receiver was located and how it operated, so that he could listen to some Western news programs. But he warned Carter not to snoop around the office.

"I mean it when I say this, Monsieur Carter. I have many secrets here, and they all are wired with some very nasty surprises . . . all of them fatal."

"I'll be careful," Carter had said. And he had been. Before lunch he had found the plastique and trigger mechanisms for the desk drawers, for the shortwave transmitter cabinet, and for three of the four hidden file cabinets. He had gotten through two of the last file cabinet's interlocking trigger mechanisms, and he knew there'd be more. Avorix had many secrets, but his most cherished were evidently in the final file drawers.

Avorix called in at three o'clock and told Carter that

progress was being made with his deal, but that it would take a little longer than expected. He said he'd be back sometime after dark.

Carter attacked the man's office with a vengeance then, finding three more trigger mechanisms for the file cabinet. For just a minute he had the urge to cross-connect all the devices, but then he had to remind himself that Avorix was a friend, not the enemy.

The file cabinet, after all of that, contained little of value. There were a number of diagrams of various Libyan military establishments, the wiring and encoding diagram for a Russian-built automatic identification unit that was installed in all Libyan Air Force planes, and the transcript of an interrogation Avorix conducted of a Sicilian Mafia leader working a drug-smuggling deal here in Tripoli.

Disappointed, he replaced the files in their proper order and reset all the trigger mechanisms, then poured himself a drink and went to the window.

The off-loading of the ship had progressed very fast, and from what Carter could see, it was nearly finished.

He stood by the window for at least an hour watching the comings and goings of the dock crews until finally they began leaving, waving good night to each other.

By 5:00 the docks were fairly quiet up and down the quay, and by 5:30 nothing moved below. Suddenly Carter was feeling very exposed. There was no reason for him *not* to trust Avorix, and yet . . .

He looked at the door, then back down at the dock. Everyone had gone for the day. If the police came and arrested him, no one would know. Avorix could claim he knew nothing—he was off doing the American's bidding— and sooner or later it would all blow over.

There was no reason for him to suspect anything of the

sort, nor was there anywhere in the city he could run to and be reasonably safe. But this place was very definitely getting on his nerves.

He finished his drink, then turned on Avorix's answering machine to the record-message mode. "I'll contact you here at ten," he said, and he rewound the tape and set the machine to answer the incoming call. If someone other than Avorix called, they'd not understand the message. There was a slight risk involved, but not a big one.

At the door he listened for any sounds from the outer office. It was quiet. He shut off the lights, opened the door, and stepped out. Avorix's secretary was seated at her desk reading a French fashion magazine. She looked up, startled, her eyes wide, just as surprised at seeing Carter as he was of seeing her.

"Good evening," he said.

"Monsieur," she replied in a small voice. "You are to remain in the office."

"I think not," Carter said. He went to the windows that looked down into the warehouse. The girl jumped up.

"Please, monsieur, it means my job."

The warehouse was deserted. Only a few small nightlights were on. He turned back to the girl. "You were supposed to watch me? Make sure I didn't take off?"

She nodded uncertainly.

Carter smiled. "Fine. I'm getting out of here, and you can come along and watch me. Any ideas where I might go to wait for Claude?"

"You are supposed . . . to stay here . . ."

"I'm not going to stay here. I am leaving. You may come or you may stay," Carter said. If Avorix was on the level after all, Carter would make sure the girl did not lose her job. If he wasn't—if he were playing a double cross—then the girl would be much better off not working for him.

He went to the door, opened it, and looked downstairs. He glanced back. "Coming?"

She looked around wildly, then grabbed her sweater, her purse, and the magazine, and followed him out the door, locking it behind her.

Carter went down the stairs and started for the side door, but the girl called after him.

"Monsieur Mentoir."

Carter turned back.

"Do you know Tripoli? Do you have an idea where you would like to go, to wait for Monsieur Avorix?"

"No," Carter admitted. "But I won't stay here."

"May I ask why?"

Carter shrugged. "I don't trust your boss. Not fully. I would prefer to wait somewhere for him that he does not control."

Marie smiled. "I understand," she said. "Then come with me. My car is in the back." She turned and headed toward a back door.

"Where are we going?" Carter asked, starting after her.

"My apartment," she said over her shoulder.

Her car was a small Renault, clean and well maintained. They headed off the quay and went a dozen blocks through town, then pulled down a side street and parked at the rear of a high-rise apartment building that overlooked the sea. It wasn't the most luxurious of neighborhoods, but like the girl and her car, it was neat and very well maintained.

Her small apartment was on the corner of the fifth floor. From one side she could look across the city of a quarter of a million people, and from the other, across the harbor to the blue Mediterranean beyond.

"Very nice," he said, standing in the middle of the living room. "You live here alone?"

She nodded. "There is wine in the kitchen. Please help yourself while I change my clothes."

She disappeared into the bedroom, and Carter went into the kitchen where he found several bottles of good red wine in the cabinet, and a few bottles of a nice Pouilly-Fuissé in the refrigerator.

He opened one of the bottles of red wine, and brought the bottle and two glasses back into the living room, where he had spotted a stereo and a rack of LPs. They were mostly classical. He put on a Brahms concerto and poured them each a glass of wine. Then he pulled off his jacket, stuffed his Luger and holster into a pocket, kicked off his shoes, and sat down on the carpeted floor, leaning back against the couch.

She came out a few minutes later, her long, jet black hair flowing down her back. She was wearing an old, faded T-shirt and a pair of denim shorts, a highly unusual, very Western outfit for this part of the world.

She smiled. "Needless to say I don't go outside dressed like this," she said to a surprised Carter in accent-free English. She came across the room and took the glass of wine he had poured for her. "Thanks," she said, and she went into the kitchen.

Carter remained where he was, bewildered, staring at the doorway. This young woman was more than she seemed to be.

She was back a few minutes later with a small tray of hors d'oeuvres, which she placed on the coffee table. She sat down cross-legged on the floor next to him.

"My name is Marie Arlemont. My parents were French, but I was born and grew up in Philadelphia. I spent my summers in France with grandparents and went to college in

Paris at the Sorbonne. When I graduated I joined my parents who had moved to Monaco. I was hired by the SDECE five years ago, and I've been out here working with Avorix for the past eighteen months.''

Hawk hadn't known about her, or he hadn't considered her important enough to mention. ''Is Avorix on the level?''

''Do you mean, is he a double? I don't know. That's why I was sent out here. Once upon a time he was the very best. His stuff lately is less than grade four.''

''And me?'' Carter asked. ''What do you know?''

''Your real name is Nicholas Carter and you work for U.S. intelligence, although for which branch I couldn't find out. State Department, I'd guess. Certainly not the Company.''

Carter had to smile.

''I've been able to get through everything except his A source file. Did you find anything?''

''You watched me?''

''Everything in there is silently alarmed.''

''Video recorders?''

''Nothing that sophisticated. Just a tape recorder.'' She drank some of her wine. ''So now you're looking for the man who ran the infamous Edri el Kebir. Then what?''

''That depends on what he has to say to me.''

She thought about that for a moment. ''You do realize that once you approach Kebir's control, no matter what is said or done, the clock will begin running on you at that moment. Kaddafi's people are pretty efficient in this. You'll have to leave Libya tonight. And so will I. Avorix is not a stupid man. He will know what has happened and who helped you. I will have to go.''

Carter was beginning to like this woman. She seemed very self-sufficient. She seemed to know exactly who she was and what she was all about. ''You have a bolt hole?''

She nodded. ''I have hidden a helicopter outside of the

city. Not too far from here. It has sufficient range to make Sicily, which is about three hundred miles.''

Carter sat up. ''A helicopter? How in hell did you manage that?''

''It wasn't easy, let me tell you. It took a lot of money, three months of work, and a lot of nervous nights. But it's there.''

''You have a pilot?''

She laughed. ''I'm the pilot, of course.''

She fixed them a light dinner, and afterward Carter took a quick shower and laid down to get some rest before he telephoned Avorix.

It was a couple of minutes before ten when she came into the bedroom, sat on the side of the bed, and shook him awake.

''It's time to call Avorix,'' she said. She had evidently taken a shower. Her hair was up in a towel, and she was wearing a bathrobe. She smelled of perfumed soap.

Carter looked at his watch. ''Go ahead and dial his number. I'll talk with him.''

She did, then handed him the receiver. Avorix answered on the first ring.

''What did you find out for me?'' Carter asked.

''That was a very stupid thing you did, Monsieur Carter. Where are you telephoning from?''

''What have you got for me?''

''Come here to my office.''

''No. Someplace else.''

''What is the matter with you?'' the Frenchman shouted. ''Don't you trust me?''

''I don't trust your office. It's probably being watched. Where can we meet, away from there?''

Avorix was silent. Marie had pulled out a dark pullover

and dark slacks from her closet and laid them over a chair.

"The main highway toward Zwara. Do you have transportation?"

"Yes."

"Five miles outside of the city. Just past the oil storage tanks. I have a Mercedes. Tan. It will be parked at the side of the road."

"When I pass I will blink twice, and you can follow me," Carter said. "What time?"

Avorix sputtered, but finally he calmed down enough to tell Carter he would be there at midnight. Earlier would be too dangerous.

Carter hung up and was about to get out of bed, when Marie opened her bathrobe and let it fall from her shoulders to the floor. She undid the towel from her hair, then came over to the bed and helped Carter out of his clothes.

"It's been a long year and a half here, Nick," she said huskily as she came into his arms. . . .

Before they left Marie bound her breasts tightly against her chest, and pinned her hair up so that when she pulled her black watch cap low on her forehead, she could be mistaken for a slightly built man or a boy.

At the door to her apartment she hesitated only a moment to look back. There was nothing personal here, she had told Carter. No photographs, no letters or favorite books, nothing that would tell anyone she was anything more than the secretary to the owner of a French import-export firm.

It had been an empty life for her these last eighteen months. When she turned and they headed downstairs to her car, her step was light. Carter was sure she was happy to be leaving here.

No one was on the back streets, but when they made it downtown there still was some traffic. Carter drove in case they were stopped. He figured he would more easily pass a police scrutiny than she would.

The night was cool, and within a few minutes they had made it to the outskirts of the city; beyond, they could see the lights outlining the tank farm.

Carter pulled his Luger out of his holster, checked to make sure there was a round in the firing chamber, and laid the weapon beside him on the seat.

Marie had a little .380 Beretta automatic. She levered a round into the chamber and held the weapon below the level of the window.

Just beyond the oil tank farm, parked at the side of the highway, was a tan Mercedes 300D. As Carter passed, he blinked the headlights twice.

The Mercedes's lights came on, and the car pulled out onto the highway. If there was going to be any trouble, it would happen now, Carter thought. But there were no other vehicles behind or ahead of them, nor was there anything in the air. Avorix was evidently playing it straight. Or at least he hadn't brought anyone with him.

About five miles farther up the coast, Carter slowed down and pulled off to the side of the road. He left the car running, grabbed Wilhelmina, and hurried back to Avorix who had pulled up just behind him.

The Frenchman seemed very nervous. "I don't understand why suddenly you no longer trust me," he said.

"What have you got set up for me?" Carter asked, a hard edge to his voice. He made no effort to conceal the Luger. Avorix kept glancing nervously at it.

"That is my secretary's automobile," Avorix said. He seemed disappointed. He looked up again at Carter. "I have arranged a very private meeting tonight for you."

"With whom?"

"Captain Waddam. He is in the Air Force, but more

importantly he is an assistant minister of defense.''

"What kind of a meeting?" Carter snapped.

"Captain Waddam, I have found out, has, shall we say, certain peculiar tastes for his recreational activities.''

"He's gay?"

"A sadomasochist. I told him about you. About your looks. Your build. He insisted on seeing you tonight.''

"Alone.''

"*Naturellement.*"

"We will follow you," Carter said, and Avorix nearly jumped out of his skin.

"Marie . . . is with you?"

"Yes," Carter said. "But we won't be there long. She can remain out of sight in the car.''

"If he has guards tonight, they certainly will not let a woman into the compound at this hour of the night.''

"They won't know she's a woman," Carter said. "We'll follow you." He turned, went back to the Renault, and got in behind the wheel.

Avorix pulled back up to the highway and headed down the road. Carter followed him.

"What has he set up?" Marie asked.

"I'm the blind date of an assistant minister of defense.''

EIGHT

On the way out, Carter explained to Marie what Avorix had set up for him, and she laughed.

"He'll be very surprised when he finds out what's in store for him. But that means Claude's position here will be exposed."

Carter had been thinking about just that. "He's planning something. He'll either kill the man, or—"

"He'll kill you and save the day for Waddam, thus solidifying his position with the Libyans," she finished.

"It's a thought," Carter said, glancing over at her. Their eyes met and she smiled nervously.

"At any rate, the helicopter is not far inland from here. We at least came in the right direction."

The Mercedes turned off the highway and continued slowly along a narrow paved road that led over a series of sand dunes toward the sea. Carter followed, and within a mile they came to an area of huge estates, all facing the Mediterranean. Each was fenced off from the road, and although some apparently were secured only by locked gates, Avorix pulled up at one where the main gate was manned by an armed guard.

The guard came up to the Mercedes, and he and Avorix

spoke for a minute or so. Once the guard looked up, switched on his flashlight, and pointed it back at the Renault. Finally something changed hands, and the guard sauntered to the gate and slowly swung it open.

Avorix drove the rest of the way inside, and as Carter passed with the Renault, the guard looked in at him. There was a disgusted expression on his face.

Inside, the road curved to the left, then up to the huge house. Avorix parked his Mercedes in front of the entryway, and Carter parked behind him but with the Renault's hood angled out; if they had to get out in a hurry, they would not be blocked by the Mercedes.

"I'm not going to be long," Carter told Marie. "I want you to get behind the wheel and be ready to take off the minute I come running."

Avorix had gotten out of the Mercedes.

"Be careful, Nick," Marie said. "Remember, we have a date in Monaco."

He got out of the car and went up to where Avorix was waiting for him. The Frenchman was out of breath.

"You are going to have to kill him when it is over. And then you are going to have to take that foolish girl with you out of Libya. Immediately!"

Avorix might have been a very good operative at one time, but now he was a frightened little man, apparently more concerned about his own welfare and his position in Tripoli than the work he was supposed to be doing.

"You've been here before," Carter said.

Avorix nodded, after a hesitation. "I bring him boys, mostly from our ships, and he gives me information."

"Edri el Kebir is a big name here. Why hadn't you gotten something on him earlier?"

"I didn't know until a week or so ago that Waddam was Kebir's control officer . . . and lover. I swear it."

Carter looked up at the imposing mansion. "Any guards inside?"

"No," Avorix said. "They come in shifts from the army base just outside the city. There are staff in the house, though. Cook, a couple of servants, a gardener."

"Let's get this over with," Carter said. He and Avorix went up the walk, and the Frenchman let them in the front door.

Just inside, they found themselves in a huge entry hall, dimly lit from above by recessed lighting. Water flowed from a fountain set in the middle of a lush tangle of plants at the center of the entry hall.

"Follow me," Avorix said, leading Carter to a grand stairway to the second floor. They walked down a long, plushly carpeted corridor, then Avorix knocked at a wide, ornately carved wooden door and shoved it open.

Waddam's master suite was huge and was open to the Mediterranean breezes along the entire front of the house except for a wall of sheer silk curtains that moved softly, almost as if they were alive.

"Is that you . . . Claude?" someone asked in French from across the room.

"*Oui,*" Avorix said. "I have brought someone to meet you."

"Good."

Avorix and Carter moved across the vast suite to a huge bed covered with black satin sheets and which faced the sea. In the center of the bed, nude, was a huge man, rolls of fat cascading down his body from massive double chins to elephantine thighs. His hands looked more like ham hocks than human limbs.

Waddam was grinning broadly. "Isn't he a lovely one," he said, slurring his words. He had been drinking red wine and some of it had dribbled down his chin onto pendulous, hairy breasts. "Come a little closer. I won't hurt you . . . yet."

Carter's stomach was churning. He stepped closer, then pulled out his Luger, which he pointed directly at the obese man's head.

Waddam moved much faster than Carter would have supposed possible for this whale of a man, rolling over and reaching out for a telephone console beside the bed.

Carter lunged forward, smashing the barrel of the Luger across the man's fingers. Waddam cried out in pain, fell back, then looked up as Carter knelt on the bed, the Luger pressed against his skull.

"And now we will talk," Carter said in French.

Waddam's eyes darted to Avorix. "Is this your doing? Are you scaring me too? Tell me . . ."

Avorix had turned away and was going toward the balcony.

"Edri el Kebir," Carter said softly.

Waddam's eyes went wide, and his complexion turned pasty.

"He is dead in a tunnel beneath the soccer stadium in Riyadh. I was with him when he died. We talked."

Waddam was whimpering.

"We talked about the Zero-hour Strike Force."

Waddam tried to press back farther into the bed. "I know nothing! Why do you come to me? Who are you?"

"You were Edri el Kebir's lover. You were his control. You sent him to Riyadh. Why? What was he doing there?"

"You are an Israeli? A Zionist?"

"Why did you send him to Riyadh? Was it to coordinate Colonel Kaddafi's nuclear strike on the oil fields?"

"No! No! You have it all wrong! It was not Libyans who made the attack. It was someone else. Kebir was just observing for us."

"What was he doing in Riyadh?"

"He had not yet reported back . . ."

"You didn't know your man was in the Saudi capital?" Carter pressed. "You'll have to do better than that."

Waddam looked around in desperation, his eyes rolling, sweat forming all over his grossly bloated body. "I knew he would be going there. But I didn't know he had arrived."

"Where had he been before Riyadh?"

"Tehran," Waddam said fearfully.

"Tehran?" Carter said. He had been there a few years ago on another assignment. "What was he doing there?"

Waddam said nothing.

"What was he doing there?" Carter repeated. "What's the connection between Riyadh and Tehran?"

Still Waddam held his silence.

"What did Kebir find out for you in Tehran? And what made you send him there in the first place?"

"Not there first. He followed someone there."

"Who?"

"I don't know. He didn't know."

"What was his starting point? What did you send him out after? What did you want to know?"

"He was in Muscat, then Doha, and Abu Dhabi first."

They were the capital cities of Oman, Qatar and the United Arab Emirates. All oil kingdoms. "Why there?"

"We had heard rumors," Waddam said. "I sent Kebir to find out what he could."

"What is the Zero-hour Strike Force? What does that mean? Whose force is it?"

"No!" Waddam screamed. He batted the Luger aside and with a powerful thrust shoved Carter off the bed. He rolled the rest of the way across the satin and grabbed the phone, but before he could bring it to his lips Avorix had come from the balcony, a silenced pistol in his hand. He fired one shot, blowing the back of Waddam's head off, blood, bits of bone, and white tissue spraying up against the wall and the leather-covered headboard.

Waddam flopped forward, knocking his face against the front of the telephone console.

Avorix pulled the receiver from beneath the dead man and brought it to his ear. Apparently no connection had been made, because he pulled out his handkerchief, wiped his fingerprints from the instrument, and set it back in its cradle.

Carter had picked himself up and held the Luger loosely at his side. The safety, however, was off.

Avorix turned to him, the silenced pistol pointing in Carter's general direction. In the dim light Carter could see that the hammer was not cocked. It would take the man a crucial split second to cock the weapon before it would be ready to fire.

"You have caused a great deal of trouble, Monsieur American Intelligence Agent," he said.

"I will kill you long before you fire your weapon, Avorix. Please believe me," Carter said.

Something flashed in the man's eyes and Carter started to bring up his Luger, when Avorix's head snapped back, his right eye disappearing in a splash of blood at the same instant the sharp crack of an automatic came from the doorway.

Carter was around in a crouch, his Luger up and ready to fire before Avorix hit the floor.

Marie stood just within the doorway, her .380 Beretta in her right hand. She too stood in a crouch, a very slight smile on her lips.

Carter swore softly to himself.

He looked back at Avorix, but it was obvious the man was dead.

A siren started up below in the compound. The shot must have been heard by the guards on staff.

"Cover the door!" Carter snapped, and he leaped to Avorix's body, searching the man's pockets until he came up with the keys to the Mercedes. The Renault would be too light to crash through the heavy steel mesh gate outside, and it was too slow if and when the Army decided to come after them.

Marie was halfway down the stairs when Carter emerged from Waddam's suite in a dead run, skidded, and nearly tripped on the thick carpeting, then raced headlong down the stairs.

The guard from the gate burst through the front door, his rifle at the ready.

Without pausing, Carter brought his Luger up and fired twice, the first shot catching the man in the throat, the second in his chest, slamming him backward out the door and onto the walkway.

"The Mercedes!" Carter shouted as he and Marie leaped over the guard's body. Carter raced around to the driver's side and had the car started as Marie climbed in.

He slammed it in gear and spun the wheel around, then jammed the accelerator to the floor. The powerful car shot around the curved driveway and back to the main gate, the siren rising and falling behind them.

"Brace yourself!" he shouted just before they hit the wire mesh gate. They burst through it, cracking the windshield and badly shoving the front of the car inward.

Fluid from the radiator immediately began to leak out as the car accelerated toward the highway.

"How far?" he asked.

"About five miles," Marie said, looking over her shoulder back toward Waddam's house. There were a lot of lights coming on in the other compounds along the road. It wouldn't be long before the Army would be out here in full force.

Five miles. It would be a testimony to Mercedes engineering if the car made it.

At the main highway Marie directed him to turn left, back toward Tripoli, and he did so without appreciably slowing down, the car slewing way to the right, nearly off the road, before he regained control.

The speedometer crept upward toward the two-hundred-kilometer-per-hour mark, and within a mile the temperature gauge was already climbing up into the red.

"There's a turnoff to the right just before the oil tank farm," Marie said.

Carter glanced in the rearview mirror. No one was following them yet. If the Army were already on their trail, he did not think he would have enough lead time for Marie to get the helicopter ready for takeoff.

The oil tank farm came into sight in the distance, and Marie motioned for Carter to slow down. "Just beyond the power lines. To the right. The road runs parallel to them."

Carter jammed on the brakes, the big car slowing to less than fifty, and he made the turn onto the narrow dirt track.

Immediately he accelerated, then turned off the headlights. For a few seconds he couldn't see a thing, but then he could make out the road stretching ahead of them as the temperature gauge continued into the red, the needle finally pegging, steam coming out of the ruins of the radiator.

"There they go," Marie said. She was looking back toward the highway.

Carter glanced in the rearview mirror in time to see a dozen sets of headlights racing down the highway from Tripoli. There were more in the distance, coming from town. It wouldn't be long before they began a search pattern, which would include this road. And if they suspected that Waddam's assassins had escaped by air, they'd send up their fighter-interceptors.

The odor of burning oil was becoming very strong in the car, and their speed was noticeably dropping, when Marie pointed out a collection of low, fallen-down stone buildings a few hundred yards off the dirt road.

Carter turned that way, the Mercedes slamming over the heavy ruts and deep sand.

Something deep within the engine suddenly began to screech loudly, the speed dropped off, and suddenly the car bucked three or four times, coming to a stop. It was the end of the line.

Marie was out of the car and racing across the desert to the largest of the buildings of what apparently at one time had been some sort of military compound. Possibly from World War II.

Carter caught up with her as she got to the building and began pulling large pieces of corrugated metal from its side wall.

Immediately Carter could see the gleam of new metal inside, and of plastic. Within a minute he could see that it was a helicopter, a fairly new design by Dessault, the French jet aircraft manufacturer. How she had gotten it here was a complete mystery, despite what she had told him back at her apartment.

It took them another five minutes to get all the corrugated metal away from the wide opening, then they ducked inside where Marie pulled the cocks out from the wheels, and the machine began to slowly roll outside. It had been put up on a small incline so that it would roll easily out into the open. She had thought of everything.

Once the machine was clear of the building, Marie untied the straps holding the rotors in place, then pulled several thick foam rubber plugs out of the various air intakes and oil cooler orifices.

Carter pulled the protective tarp off the plastic bubble

windshield and tossed it back inside the building. As Marie climbed into the chopper to get it ready for takeoff, Carter shoved the sheets of corrugated metal back in place so that no one coming by here would know that anything had been taken out recently. Not unless they stopped, pulled the tin aside, and looked in.

By the time he was finished, the rotor blades were beginning to spin, the engines catching. He climbed aboard and strapped himself in. Marie had one earphone on, and she looked over at him and winked.

"The Air Force hasn't been called out yet. All we need is ten minutes, maybe fifteen, and we'll be clear."

Gradually she brought the throttle up and eased the rotor pitch so that the big blades bit deeper into the cool desert air. They lifted off gently, and at about fifty feet they turned toward the north, Marie bringing the machine to full throttle, just skimming the desert.

Carter was about to ask her if she remembered the power lines, but they were already over them. She skirted to the west of the tank farm before dropping down again and heading north. Soon they were out over the water.

Marie stiffened in her seat and glanced over at Carter.

"They asking about us?" he guessed.

She nodded. "Tripoli Military Control is demanding us to stand down. They've lost us—we're too low."

"They'll be coming out after us," Carter said, looking over his shoulder, back the way they had come. The lights of Tripoli were spread out to the east.

"How far will they come out?"

"Twelve miles, maybe more. Hard to tell after our Navy shot down their planes in '81. But they'll be coming after us with jets."

"We'll see just how good they are," Marie said, and she dipped the helicopter down in a sickening lurch to within a few feet of the waves, which, as far as Carter could tell, had built into eight- and ten-footers. They were skimming just over the tops of them, leaving a spray behind.

The machine was doing well over a hundred miles per hour, and Carter estimated they were not more than ten or twelve feet above the tops of the highest waves. Marie was much better than a good pilot, he realized. She was one of the best.

"They're on their way," she said suddenly, not looking up from what she was doing. "A pair of fighter-interceptors. They're coming after us with orders to shoot us down if we don't turn around."

Carter alternately watched her and the sky overhead. For a long time there was nothing except the drone of the helicopter engine and the waves shooting past just beneath them.

"One of the pilots thinks he's spotted us," Marie said. "They're coming down to take a look." She immediately slowed the machine down and came around into the moving trough of one of the waves. For half a minute or more she jockeyed the controls back and forth until she had the chopper settled into the wave trough, moving sideways in line with it.

A jet fighter flashed overhead at about five hundred feet, then screamed out toward the horizon, making a wide looping turn to the east.

Instantly Marie popped up out of the wave trough, cranked in full throttle, and they accelerated toward the north.

Sweat shimmered off her brow as she concentrated. "He couldn't find us," she announced triumphantly. "He's making another pass."

Once again she dropped down into a wave trough, but this time she stabilized the chopper's speed and drift much more quickly.

The jet screamed overhead, lower than the last time, but Marie held her position, the waves at times towering over them. If one of the crests broke, or if she miscalculated by the slightest amount, tons of water would come cascading down on top of them. They'd never know what hit them.

The jet screamed past them about a half mile to the north.

Marie maintained their position, but finally she broke out into a grin and pulled the helicopter up out of the trough, this time turning to the northwest.

When she had gained enough altitude that her control wasn't so critical, she looked over at Carter and pulled off her earphones and the attached microphone.

"I hope you know someone aboard the *Forrestal*," she said, handing the headset to Carter.

"Our aircraft carrier?"

"She's out there, and she's scrambled four of her fighter-interceptors to see what our Libyan friends were up to."

Carter took the headset and put it on. He could hear the chatter between the Libyan pilots and their controller. But in the background he could hear the American pilots speaking with their ship.

"Red leader, this is Red Dog one. We pick something coming up out of the clutter bearing one-seven-niner."

"Heading out?"

"That's a roger, Red leader. Slow . . . hold one . . . it's a chopper, I think."

Carter keyed the microphone. "That's affirmative, *Forrestal*. This is Commander Nick Carter aboard a Dessault helicopter. We'd appreciate a little help."

"Did you copy that, Red leader?"

"That's a roger, Red Dog one. Keep tracking, we're checking." There was a silence until the *Forrestal* was back. "Did he say Commander Nick Carter?"

"I think so," one of the pilots said.

"Affirmative," Carter said into the mike. "Request permission to land aboard."

"Permission granted, Commander. Do you need vectors?" the *Forrestal* radioman asked.

Carter was about to say yes when he spotted the lights of the gigantic aircraft carrier on the horizon. Swarming overhead were the lights of four fast-moving jet fighters.

"That's a negative, *Forrestal*. We have you in sight," Carter said. "I'll turn you over to my pilot for landing instructions."

"Roger."

Carter handed the headset back to Marie, who pulled it on. "I've never landed on an aircraft carrier before," she said.

"There's a first time for everything," Carter said with a grin.

NINE

Carter and Marie were escorted immediately up to the admiral's quarters just below the bridge deck, where Admiral Richard Brewster himself was waiting with his executive officer, Captain Howard Baker.

They were both astounded that the helicopter's pilot was a woman, but they were even more surprised to learn that she had been born in America, was now a citizen of Monaco, and worked for the SDECE.

"This is just a bit unusual, Commander Carter," the admiral said. "But we were told you were in the area and were alerted to provide any assistance we could if and when the need arose. We were not told about a woman."

"I'll need to use your crypto facilities, and I'm sure Mademoiselle Arlemont will want to report to her superiors," Carter said.

"We'll set up a circuit for you, Commander," the admiral said, "But Miss Arlemont's message will either have to wait until she returns home or will have to go through the State Department. Policy, I'm afraid."

"I'll wait," Marie said. She turned to Carter. "Just tell

your people exactly what happened, especially regarding Avorix. They'll pass that along to Paris."

Carter nodded. "Where is this ship bound, Admiral?" he asked.

"Nowhere in particular. We're merely here to show our nuclear presence in case something heats up," the admiral said. "We can get Miss Arlemont to Athens if she wishes to get to Paris. That would be the quickest way."

"That's fine," Marie said.

"And you, Commander?"

"Tehran, I think."

The executive officer started to say something, but the admiral cut him off. "Shall we go up to communications?"

"Yes," Carter said. He turned to Marie. "I'll see you later."

Captain Baker escorted Marie to her quarters on level five while the admiral went with Carter up to the bridge deck, where aft they were admitted through a series of security checks and finally into the tiny encrypted communications center, off the main comm facility.

There were four teletype crypto units along with one facsimile device, all linked by satellite to the Pentagon. On the admiral's orders, the operator cleared out, and Carter punched in the routing codes that within a few minutes connected him with Hawk on Dupont Circle.

As quickly and succinctly as possible, Carter explained how he made it from Riyadh to Tripoli, his connection with Claude Avorix, the help Marie Arlemont had given him and her suspicions about Avorix, and the events at Waddam's estate. He typed:

PLAN TO PROCEED TO ATHENS FROM
THERE DIRECT ON GREEK AIRLINES TO
TEHRAN. COVER MARCEL MENTOIR,

FRENCH OIL EQUIPMENT PUMPING
SALESMAN. REQUEST SUPPORTING
DOCUMENTS, SPECIFICATION, BOOKS,
AND ORDER FORMS DELIVERED TO ME AT
ATHENS HELLENIKON AIRPORT NLT . . .

Carter hesitated. "What is our ETA Athens, Admiral?"
It was after four in the morning. "We can have you there
by helicopter at the airport before midnight."
Carter turned back to the teletype.

. . . 2300 HOURS THIS DATE. ALSO
REQUESTING 9MM AMMUNITION,
CLOTHING, AND LUGGAGE. FINALLY,
REQUESTING MY WEAPONS BE
IMMEDIATELY SENT WITH OIL EQUIPMENT
SPECIFICATION BOOKS AND MATERIALS
VIA DIPLOMATIC POUCH TO FRENCH
EMBASSY TEHRAN.

The admiral had been watching the monitor, and he whistled. Carter looked up.
"This is all Q-category top secret, Admiral," Carter said,
a hard edge to his voice. It was the admiral's ship, so Carter
could hardly have asked him to leave. But he could damned
well make the man understand the importance of what was
happening here.
"Aye-aye," the man said.

WORKING.

Hawk had teletyped the single word to let Carter know that his requests were being arranged and to stand by.

"How long will this take?" the admiral asked.

Carter shrugged. "No way of telling. An hour, maybe more."

The admiral got to his feet. "I don't know about you, Commander, but I'm going to get myself a drink. Can I bring you anything?"

"Yes, sir," Carter said. "A bottle of cognac and a pack of cigarettes."

"I think that can be arranged."

"Listen, Admiral, I want to thank you for helping us. We were in a bit of a tight spot with those Libyan jets back there."

The admiral chuckled. "We can't let the *Nimitz* have all the fun," he said as he left.

Carter sat back and reread everything he had sent to Hawk. *Zero-hour Strike Force*. The words had an ominous ring to them and seemed even more deadly by being in print in a place like this. But what the hell had Waddam heard that made him send his top spy to Muscat, and Abu Dhabi, and Tehran, and finally Riyadh among the other oil capitals? He said he had heard rumors. What sort of rumors? That an oil field would be attacked? It would explain why Kebir had visited each capital. But if that were the case, Carter's going to Tehran would accomplish nothing. The attack had been on Saudi Arabia.

There were other possibilities though, Carter thought. It was possible that Saudi Arabia was only the first target. Other attacks could come.

But by whom? The Zero-hour Strike Force was apparently some sort of commando group. The men that had swooped down on the Saudi desert in Israeli planes and with Israeli equipment . . .

Strike that.

He sat forward. The aircraft had been reported as Hercules C-130s. American-built. Our forces used such equipment. We had sold many of the planes to Israel and to other countries as well. But there hadn't been hundreds of thousands of those planes built and sold; the number was relatively small. It would not be outside the realm of possibility to find out where every C-130 ever built was located and to find out exactly where they were on that morning that the bombs were delivered.

They wouldn't be able to find out about all the planes, of course, but they'd be able to narrow the field down considerably.

He turned back to the teletype and sent out his request, outlining exactly what he wanted done and the reasons he wanted the information.

When he was finished, the admiral was back with a bottle of Martel cognac, a couple of snifters, and a pack of cigarettes. Before the officer could get a look at the monitor or the prime set on which Carter had been working, Carter jumped up and tore out the last message, then burned it in a wastepaper can.

The admiral watched him. "That sensitive?"

"Yes, sir," Carter said. He didn't really know why he had destroyed that part of the message before the admiral could see it, but something deep inside his gut, or way at the back of his brain, was beginning to nag at him, was beginning to worry him.

The teletype came alive a half hour later:

ALL TERMS ARRANGED. KIMITRI
MOUDHROS WILL MEET YOU AT
2300 HOURS THIS DATE HELLENIKON
AIRPORT. THANKS TO MISS ARLEMONT.
GOOD LUCK TO YOU.
/signed/ HAWK

Carter knew Móudhros; he was the Amalgamated Press and Wire Services chief of station for Athens, which included operations in the Balkan countries. He was a good man, if a little overemotional. And he looked a lot like Telly Savalas. He was a real ladies' man. Carter liked him.

Carter took the teletype paper from both machines and destroyed it, then finished his drink and stubbed out his cigarette.

The admiral got up. "I imagine you must be tired. I'll walk back down with you and show you to your quarters."

"Thanks, but I think I'll stay up a while longer," Carter said. "Why don't you just point me in the direction of Miss Arlemont's quarters?" He grabbed the bottle of cognac on his way out.

It was just a little before 11:00 P.M. when Carter and Marie touched down at the business aviation terminal of Athens's Hellenikon Airport in the Dessault helicopter. The *Forrestal*'s maintenance crew had made sure the machine was in good working order and had gassed her up.

Just northwest of Crete, about 150 air miles south of Athens, they had lifted off for the uneventful night flight over the Mirtoön Sea.

They had made love slowly, gently, and with much feeling in the early morning hours aboard the aircraft carrier, and then had fallen asleep in each other's arms.

Carter had awoken around noon, had gone down to the officers' mess, and spent the afternoon on the bridge until dinner, when he and Marie were guests at the admiral's table.

That evening they made sure the helicopter was ready, and just before ten they lifted off.

Marie made arrangements with the terminal manager to put the chopper into short-term storage. Someone would come for it soon, she said. Then she and Carter were processed through customs, and outside—she waiting for a cab to go into the city and he getting set to climb aboard the shuttle over to the main terminal—they kissed.

"Take care of yourself," she said.

"I'll try."

"Maybe I should tag along . . ."

"I'll see you in Monaco," Carter said firmly. He kissed her again, then climbed onto the shuttle. She waved sadly as the little bus left the curb.

Kimi Móudhros was waiting at the newsstand inside the main terminal, his back against a support column, his nose buried in the Paris edition of the *Herald-Tribune*.

"Ah-ha, Marcel," he boomed, tossing the paper in a trashcan. "How good to see you again." He gripped Carter in a bear hug, making no attempt to make their meeting covert. "I think we are being watched," he whispered in English into Carter's ear.

"It's good to see you too, *mon ami*," Carter said loudly in French.

Móudhros grabbed Carter by the arm, and together they got on an elevator and went up to the parking ramp. They stepped into the shadows and waited for a full five minutes.

"I think I may have picked up a tail from town," Móudhros said softly.

"Are you working on anything important?"

"Not a thing. It is very curious; the moment I get the call about you, I acquire a tail."

"They're probably waiting at the exit," Carter said.

"Could be," Móudhros said. "Let's get you ready so you can be on your way."

They went back to where the Greek had parked his Volkswagen minibus. Curtains covered the windows. Inside, in the back, he opened a battered leather suitcase and showed

Carter the clothing that had been picked out for him.

"This you take with you. You're booked on the overnight flight into Tehran which leaves in a little more than an hour. I'm to meet the courier with the French diplomatic pouch in half an hour just outside the airport with your package. It goes out on the same flight. You'll be met in Tehran, and you will be given a briefcase. Your papers and your weapons will be in it."

Carter quickly pulled off his Luger and stiletto, and handed them over to Móudhros, who placed them in a brown leather attaché case that matched the suitcase.

"This will be the case waiting for you."

Carter felt naked without his weapons.

Móudhros handed over Carter's tickets, about a thousand dollars' worth of Iranian rials, and then stamped his French passport with the proper visa.

When he was finished, he hugged Carter and kissed him on both cheeks. "I wish you very much luck, my friend. I think I know what you are after, and I know that it is very dangerous now for an American to be anywhere within the Arab world. So be especially careful. And may Allah be with you." He laughed.

"Thanks," Carter said. He checked outside, but no one was there, so he grabbed the suitcase, shook Móudhros's hand, and hopped out of the minibus. He headed directly across the parking ramp and entered the terminal from a different doorway than the one through which they had left.

Immediately he went to the Olympic Airways counter, where he checked in and was given a boarding pass. Then he sat in the lounge, in a corner, until it was time for him to board.

They lost an hour flying east, so they landed in Tehran at 4:45 in the morning. A gigantic picture of Khoumeni hung from the side of the terminal building. It fluttered in the light morning breeze as they taxied to the parking ramp and turned inward toward the terminal building as the engines wound down.

Inside, once the baggage had come up, Carter's was searched thoroughly by a very efficient customs agent. Even the lining of the luggage was searched, and afterward he was frisked by hand as well as having to walk through a metal detector. He would never have gotten into the country with his weapons or his spare passports, he realized.

"Your name?" the customs agent asked in French.

"Marcel Mentoir."

"Nationality?"

"French."

"Reason for coming to Iran?"

"Business."

The customs agent looked up from Carter's passport. "What sort of business, Monsieur Mentoir?"

"I represent a firm that manufactures oil pumping equipment. I am here hoping to make some sales now that you have decided to begin pumping oil again."

"We have never *stopped* pumping oil, monsieur. What you may have heard were nothing more than ugly rumors," the customs agent snapped. He handed Carter's passport back after stamping the date and time in it, then motioned Carter on.

Carter went through the customs barrier and hesitated inside the terminal proper, looking for someone carrying the attaché case that matched his luggage. The diplomatic pouches would be the first items off the plane, and they would be on their way into the city by now. Whoever was to meet him here with the attaché case would have had plenty of time. But there were very few people in the terminal at this hour, and no one carried anything even remotely similar to the attaché case.

He crossed through the terminal, hesitated again by the

main doors, and looked back, but still no one had appeared.

There could have been a mix-up, he decided. If it came to that, he'd stop by the French embassy in a couple of hours and pick up his things.

Yet he felt vulnerable and very much exposed as he stepped outside and across the wide sidewalk to the curb where a half-dozen taxis and two buses were taking on passengers from the Greek airliner that had just landed.

Again, as he had twice inside, Carter stopped and surveyed the people and the luggage they carried. But still there was no sign of any Frenchman with a brown leather case that matched the single piece Carter carried.

He held back, lighting a cigarette as he waited for the rest of the passengers to come out.

A half hour later, the buses had gone and only two of the cabs remained. The driver in the lead taxi leaned out of his window and looked at Carter.

"Cheap, I will take you into town if your ride has not shown up," he said. He spoke in English.

"I think so," Carter said, his English heavily accented. He came across to the cab and got in, tossing his suitcase beside him on the seat.

"Where do you wish to go, monsieur?" the driver asked, switching into very bad French as he put the cab in gear and they headed into town.

Carter looked back as they slid away from the terminal, but no one was coming out after them. The other cab—the only other vehicle in sight—remained where it was.

"Monsieur?"

Carter turned back. "The French embassy."

"*Oui, monsieur.*"

Carter sat back and lit a cigarette as they hurried onto the main highway past the burned-out remains of what appeared to have been a gas station, then turned toward the capital city of a dying country. Khoumeni was ill, and there was more corruption, more graft, and certainly more political executions under this government than there had been under the repressive Shah's regime. Over the past eighteen months or so, there had been a steady stream of reports about the breakdown of order within the country. The war with Iraq seemed never-ending, and there were so many splinter groups—armed splinter groups—roaming the cities as well as the countryside, that much of the day-to-day business of the country would soon be grinding to a standstill. Oil exports had decreased to a trickle, which of course was blamed on faulty equipment left behind by the Americans. At the moment, the French were about the only ones left in general favor here.

They passed the broken-down hulk of an army truck turned over at the side of the road, and past the sports stadium, closed now, a farmers' market was being set up as the sun was just appearing over the horizon.

The French embassy was housed in a two-story white stucco building that had at one time been the home of some wealthy family. Tall iron gates opened into a front courtyard that led up to the main entrance of leaded glass doors with bars over them. A few trees grew in the courtyard, and the overall effect was one of peace and quiet.

The cabby dropped Carter off at the front gate, and when he was gone, Carter approached it. A button was set in the wall just below a speaker grille. A brass plaque said in French: Ring for Service.

Carter pushed the button, then looked over his shoulder down the street. A black Mercedes sedan had come around the corner and parked half a block away. There were two men inside, but he couldn't tell much more. The car had Iranian plates.

"*Oui,*" a voice came from the speaker.

Carter turned back. *"Ici Monsieur Marcel Mentoir."*

"Oui?"

"There is a package here for me," Carter said.

"I know of no package for a Monsieur Mentoir," the impersonal voice droned.

"It came this morning on the Olympic flight from Athens. In the diplomatic pouch."

"Diplomatic pouch? From Athens? *Non, monsieur.* There was no diplomatic pouch from Athens."

TEN

No diplomatic pouch. Móudhros could not be a traitor. It was impossible to believe that he could set something up like this.

"Please check with the ambassador," Carter insisted.

"I am telling you, monsieur, there is no diplomatic pouch from Athens, not this morning."

"Later today?"

"Non, monsieur. Not until next week at the earliest."

How could Kimitri have gotten it so wrong? But Móudhros had said he was being followed. Damn. They had set him up!

"A phone!" Carter shouted into the speaker. "I need to use the telephone. We must get through to Athens."

But there was no answer. Whoever he had been speaking with either had shut off the intercom or was refusing to respond.

"Please! It is urgent . . ." Carter tried again, when out of the corner of his eye he detected a movement.

He spun around just in time to avoid being hit by a shot fired by one of the men from the Mercedes. The bullet ricocheted off the concrete wall, inches from his side.

The second man in the car was getting out from behind the wheel as Carter dodged to the right.

Two more shots were fired, whining off the pavement behind him as he ducked around the corner and raced head-long down the narrow street.

It wouldn't take them very long to get back in their car and come after him. He was going to have to find a hiding place, and fast.

At the end of the block he turned left, and the street suddenly opened onto a wide, traffic-filled square. Cars, trucks, buses, and pedestrians were everywhere. He pulled up short. He did not want to be arrested by the Iranian police. If they locked him up, he'd end up like a goldfish in a bowl—anyone who wanted to take a potshot at him would have no problem.

Head down, a determined look on his face as if he were hurrying off to a business meeting, Carter walked around the square as the black Mercedes came out from the side street, paused a moment, and then turned left behind him.

He had thought that coming here to Tehran would probably prove nothing, but he had been wrong. Something very big was going on. They had apparently known that he would be contacting Móudhros. And they had arranged the diplomatic pouch thing. But how? And even more importantly, who? Certainly not the Israelis. The KGB might be able to pull something like this off, but Carter had his doubts. No, he thought, this had all the earmarks of being an American operation. But that was totally impossible. We would never have dropped nuclear weapons on Saudi Arabia. There was no reason for it.

A cop was directing traffic, and at the first corner Carter held back until there were several other people crossing the intersection with him, then he went.

A moment later the black Mercedes came through the intersection, sped up, and fifty yards ahead, the passenger door popped open and a tall, almost cadaverously thin man jumped out. His right hand was in his coat pocket.

The car shot ahead, and the tall man skipped between the parked cars, coming toward Carter. The driver would circle the block, coming up behind Carter and stopping any escape that way. But for a minute or so the two men would be out of sight of each other.

The street was fronted by a long row of shops. At that moment Carter stood in front of a small lending library, several books arranged in a display in the window. Inside, he could see an old man doing something behind a counter.

He stepped into the doorway and tried the door. It was locked, but the old man looked up and shook his head. Too early.

Carter banged on the door. The man with the gun was nearly on top of him.

The old man, exasperated now, came to the door and unlocked it. Before he could say anything, Carter pushed past him, leaped over the counter, and slipped through a narrow opening between two of the book racks.

The old man shouted something behind him, but he was cut off in mid-sentence.

Carter hurried around a stack of books and listened as the front door was closed and locked. Something was being dragged across the floor.

He reached down and slipped off his shoes, then noiselessly ducked down and moved toward the front of the shop.

The thin man had come over the counter and was coming down the same aisle Carter had used. He could see the man's head through gaps in the books.

Carefully Carter crept in front of a tall bookcase and peered around it. The armed man stood ten feet away, his back turned to him.

Without hesitation Carter straightened up, and in a couple of long strides was on top of him.

The man had started to turn around when Carter kicked his left leg out from under him, then smashed his fist into the side of the man's head as he was going down.

The pistol clattered to the floor, and Carter quickly scooped it up. It was a big .357 magnum with a short barrel to which was attached a silencer. A very effective killing machine within twenty-five or thirty yards.

The tall, thin man was dazed and was trying to get to his knees. Carter checked to make sure the pistol was loaded, then vaulted over the counter to make sure the door was locked. It was. He didn't want someone wandering in at this moment.

The elderly shopkeeper lay out of sight in the corner, his head turned at an unnatural angle, his eyes open. He was dead. The son of a bitch had killed him.

Carter went back to where the tall man was pulling himself up. His eyes were still glazed, although he was coming around. Carter was mad. It would have been so easy just to pull the trigger and get it over with, but he held himself in check by sheer will power. The other man had recovered enough to understand that. He backed away.

"Why did you have to kill the old man?" Carter hissed. "You could have just knocked him out. You didn't have to do that to him, you bastard." Carter spoke in English.

"You don't understand," the tall man said, also in English. He had a drawl. Texas? Maybe Arizona or New Mexico. Definitely an American.

Oh, hell, Carter thought, *speak anything but English. Even Hebrew, but not American English.* "Who are you and what the hell is going on?"

The man said nothing.

"Why did you try to kill me?"

"You're messing with something that's none of your concern."

"Zero-hour Strike Force?"

The tall man lunged, but Carter had seen it coming from his eyes and easily sidestepped the rush, laying open the man's cheek with the lip of the silencer.

He cocked the big pistol, and when the tall man turned back he was looking directly into the barrel. He stopped short.

"I'd just as soon blow your head off here and now for what you did to the old man up front. But first we'll talk."

The tall man's eyes glazed over as he did something with his tongue. Too late Carter realized that the man had a cyanide capsule or some other poison in a tooth. He grabbed for the man just as he collapsed.

Carter checked his pulse, but there was nothing. He was dead. He quickly went through the man's pockets, coming up with a couple of hundred dollars in Iranian rials, a penknife, a key for the Tehran Sheraton, and his wallet, which contained, among other things, a U.S. State Department identification card.

Carter stared at it for a very long time. Something seemed terribly wrong here. The card was very possibly a forgery. Or at least Carter hoped so. It identified the man as Leslie Lowell Lassiter II of Beaumont, Texas. His position was listed as special assistant to the secretary of state himself.

It has to be a forgery, Carter thought. He did not want to contemplate the consequences if it wasn't.

He pocketed Lassiter's wallet and the hotel key, then put his shoes back on and went to the front of the shop.

The black Mercedes was just passing, the driver intently looking the other way.

Carter slipped outside, locking the door behind him. He

had stuffed the .357 in his belt beneath his jacket and started up the block in the direction the Mercedes had gone.

The sun was fully up now, and with it came the heat. Pedestrian and vehicular traffic was everywhere. A cacophony of noise seemed to hover over the square.

Carter spotted the Mercedes pulled up at the curb in the next block. He quickly ducked through traffic to the other side of the street and hurried up to a spot across from the car. The driver, a short, squat man, leaned against the hood of the car watching the pedestrian traffic in the direction Carter had come from. He was clearly nervous.

There was a break in the traffic, and Carter dashed across the street. He put his right hand inside his coat, his fingers curling around the .357, and with his left he carefully opened the rear door and quickly got in.

The short man, feeling the motion of the car, spun around and looked inside at the same moment Carter pulled out the magnum and pointed it at his head.

"You'd better get in and get us out of here before I kill you," Carter said.

The man's eyes were wide. He opened the door on the passenger side, got in, and slid over behind the wheel.

"Where's Les?"

"Dead," Carter said, and the man started to turn around. "And I'll kill you as well unless you do exactly as I tell you!"

The man stopped.

"The Sheraton," Carter said. "And so help me God, if you give me any trouble, any trouble whatsoever, you won't have to use your cyanide tablet."

The man started the car, and when there was a break in traffic, he pulled smoothly away from the curb and headed across town.

It took nearly a half hour to make it to the Sheraton, a tall edifice of glass and steel that had, from what Carter remembered, seen better days. Carter directed the little man to park in the rear parking lot very close to one of the exits. After relieving the other man of his .38 Police Special, which he shoved under the seat, he pocketed the magnum, and they got out of the car.

"What are we doing here?" the little man asked.

"We're going up to eight-oh-seven," Carter said.

The little man stepped back a pace. "You don't know what the hell you're doing."

"I intend on finding out," Carter said, and he motioned for the man to head up to the hotel.

"No."

"I'll kill you."

"For what? What have I done to you?"

"I'm talking about nuclear war."

"What?"

"Zero-hour Strike Force."

The little man's eyes went wide, and he paled. "Jesus," he said softly. "Oh, Jesus Christ."

Carter stepped forward and was about to demand an explanation, when the little man pulled out a small .32-caliber automatic and fired twice, the first shot hitting Carter in the shoulder, driving him backward, and the second just grazing his side.

The little man turned, dropped the gun and the car keys, and scurried off across the parking lot. Carter dropped down into the classic shooter's stance, following the retreating figure, the .357 cocked, his finger on the trigger . . . but he could not shoot the man. He was still an American. Something very bad was happening here—had happened, was about to happen—and yet he could not pull the trigger.

He lowered the pistol and straightened up as the little man rounded the corner of the hotel and disappeared from sight.

A woman and her two children were looking his way from

the opposite side of the parking lot, and a man in the back doorway of the hotel hurriedly shut the door when Carter turned his way.

He leaped forward, scooped up the car keys and the other weapon, then hurried back to the Mercedes. He got behind the wheel, started the car, and pulled out of the parking lot and headed away from the hotel, a wave of dizziness and nausea coming over him from his wounds.

It wouldn't be very long before the Iranian police were called about the shooting. Someone had almost certainly seen him getting into the Mercedes and drive off, which meant the city would no longer be safe for him.

He turned down a quiet back street, getting away from the heavier downtown traffic, and pulled up behind a tumbledown building.

The wound in his side hurt like hell, but it was only a graze and would cause him no trouble. But his shoulder was worse. The bullet had evidently lodged just below the collarbone. There wasn't much blood, and it didn't hurt, but his entire side was numb. Later, he knew, the pain would come.

He stuffed his handkerchief over the wound and rebuttoned his shirt. Then he opened the glove compartment and looked inside. He found the car maintenance books as well as a small package that contained several thousand rials, a map of Tehran, and a road map of the entire country. A spot in Khuzistan, one of the southern provinces bordering on the Persian Gulf, was circled. Directly to the west was Iraq, but to the southwest was Kuwait, and beyond that, Saudi Arabia.

Carter stared at the circled spot on the map for several long seconds. Access to the Gulf. And certainly easy air access to Saudi Arabia.

He looked up. It made him sick at heart to think that his own government was involved with this thing. But more and more it looked as if that were the case.

But if that were so, why had he been sent out here? That did not make a lot of sense.

He looked at the map again. It was more than four hundred miles overland to Bandar Ma'Shur, the tiny village circled. The powerful automobile would make it if he could find the diesel fuel, but he did not know if he could stand up to it.

He spread the map out on the seat next to him, replaced the package with the money in the glove compartment, and pulled out of the narrow street onto the busier boulevard. Within twenty minutes he was headed southwest out of the city on a wide, well-maintained paved highway.

It was still early morning, and the full heat of the day had not built up. There was quite a bit of traffic on the highway for the first few miles out of Tehran, but gradually it thinned out, so that about fifty miles south, there was only an occasional truck.

The big car did well—at times he was doing eighty on the straight, empty stretches—so that by nine o'clock, when the pain from his shoulder wound began coming at him in waves, he was more than a hundred miles south of Tehran.

The country here was mountainous, and up from the valley the air was cool, although the driving was more difficult on the winding roads.

He skirted the city of Kashan. With its population of fifty or sixty thousand people, it maintained a vigorous police force. If the search had expanded from Tehran, no major city would be safe for him.

The road kept climbing, some of the mountain peaks around him towering to twelve and thirteen thousand feet.

At around ten o'clock the road dipped down into a small mountain town nestled in a narrow valley. Carter stopped in the main square across from a small inn and cranked down the window. A young boy of twelve or thirteen stood near the inn staring at him, his eyes very wide and dark.

Carter motioned for him to come over, and he did, eagerly, almost like a puppy. There were three other cars and two trucks parked around the main street, but there were only a few people. A couple of old men, seated at the inn, looked up and were watching.

"Do you understand French?" Carter asked the boy, but there was no response. He tried English and then German, but the boy just stared at him. Smiling.

"Fuel," Carter said. "Petrol."

Still the boy did not understand.

Moving carefully now, because he was in so much pain, Carter eased out of the car. The boy stepped back.

"Diesel fuel," Carter said, stumbling back to the gas filler. He opened the little door and pointed. "Fuel."

The boy stopped smiling, nodded, then turned and ran off down the main street. Carter watched him for a moment, then looked over at the inn. Once he had the fuel situation taken care of, he would risk going into the restaurant for something to eat. But if there was going to be any trouble here, he wanted the car fueled and ready to go first.

He went back to the front of the car and sat down in the driver's seat, but he left the door open. He lit a cigarette, and as he smoked he tried to make some sense of what he had learned so far. But it was frustrating. Everything pointed to American government involvement in the nuclear strike, yet he could not bring himself to accept it.

It was nearly fifteen minutes later when the young boy came around the corner. With him were three men, two of them each carrying a pair of jerry cans, and the third, an older man, carrying what appeared to be a black doctor's bag.

Carter got painfully out of the car as they approached.

"The boy says he thinks you are French," the doctor said in French.

"*Oui*," Carter said. "Is that diesel fuel?"

"Yes, it is, and it has been well filtered, I assure you," the doctor said. He said something to the other two men, who went to the back of the car and busied themselves filling the tank.

"You are a doctor?"

"Yes, I am, and I can see you are hurt. The boy is very worried."

"It is a gunshot wound . . . two of them, actually," Carter said. "I was set on out on the highway about fifty miles from here."

"Barbarians, all of them," the doctor said. He led Carter into the inn, where the old man who ran the place had already set out a couple of bowls of very hot water and a bottle of rough red wine.

"How did he know?" Carter asked.

"News travels very fast in this town, monsieur. We have a telephone. I called ahead."

Carter took off his jacket, then laid the .357 on the table. No one even appeared to notice it. He peeled off his shirt, and the innkeeper took it away from him and disappeared with it into the back.

"You are in pain?" the doctor asked, gently probing the shoulder wound.

"Considerable pain," Carter said.

"I will give you something to make you sleep for a few hours—"

"Just a local anesthetic," Carter interrupted.

The doctor looked into his eyes, then nodded. "As you wish."

Several people had wandered in from the square, and they sat around respectfully, drinking tea and watching wide-eyed as their local doctor repaired the wounded Frenchman who drove the very large German car.

It took nearly a half hour for the local to take effect, and even then, the doctor warned in his soft French, there would be a lot of deep pain. The bullet, he found by probing, was lodged just beneath the collarbone.

Carter took some of the wine, then nodded up at the doctor. "I have a very important appointment soon. I must not be late."

The doctor seemed amused. "I don't think you will be in any shape to travel when I have finished."

"I must," Carter said, gripping the doctor's arm with his good hand.

The doctor said nothing as his disengaged himself and began the operation.

At first there was no pain, only some dull probing and cutting sensations, but then it was as if a dentist had just drilled deeply into a raw nerve without Novocain; pain thrummed through his body making him feel like a plucked guitar string. Sweat instantly popped out over his body, and the room began to spin lazily around overhead.

The doctor was speaking to a woman who was doing something to Carter's chest with large bundles of gauze. But his voice and her ministrations seemed to be happening far away and in a different time.

At one point the doctor said something and held a dark object up in front of Carter's nose. It was held in tweezers and was easy to see, yet it took him a long time to realize it was the bullet from his shoulder.

Time seemed to accelerate then, until the room began to come into focus from where he was lying on a long table, a pillow beneath his head. It was dark outside.

He sat up, the room spinning for a moment, but then his head began to clear. He swung his feet over the edge of the table and stepped down.

It was well after ten at night according to his watch. He had been out the entire day.

He padded in stocking feet across the inn to the front windows and looked outside. The Mercedes was parked in front, its paint and chrome shining. While he had been out, the townspeople had evidently washed and shined the car.

He looked down at his shoulder and side, which were well bandaged. There was very little pain in comparison to what he had felt when he had come here. The ache was centered deep in his shoulder, but there was no longer the dull sickness from the piece of lead in his shoulder.

Laid out neatly on the chair were his jacket and shirt, both cleaned and mended, and the .357 magnum, also freshly cleaned and oiled.

He checked the weapon. It was still loaded.

Quickly he got dressed, stuffing the magnum in his belt. At the door he hesitated a moment, then came back to the counter and pulled out nearly a thousand dollars in rials, which he laid out in a neat stack.

The doctor or one of the townsmen would know best how the money should be divided.

Outside, he looked around, but the town seemed deserted. There was a full moon casting its pale glow over everything. There were no other lights. There was no one.

He got into the car, turned the key, and started the engine. The fuel gauge climbed past the full mark. Clean, well-filtered fuel, the doctor had promised.

He pulled away from the curb and headed out of town. A block or so away from the inn, he was certain he had caught a glimpse of a small boy's face in the window of one of the houses, but then he was past and he wasn't sure he had seen anything at all.

ELEVEN

Carter was a dozen miles south of the small town when he discovered that the villagers had packed him some food and a couple of bottles of mineral water. The bundle was in the back seat, and he noticed it in the rearview mirror as he adjusted it.

He drove rapidly, feeling so much better now that the bullet had been removed. At times, in straight stretches of the road, he exceeded a hundred miles per hour.

Sometime in the early morning hours he crossed the Zagros Mountains, coming down toward the vast, fertile valley that, to the west, in Iraq, was fed by the Tigris and Euphrates rivers.

He made the last 250 miles in something under four hours, coming to the Persian Gulf at around 2:00 A.M., the town of Bandar Ma'Shur a couple of miles to the east, a very few lights reflecting out into the water.

At the side of the road he drank some of the water and flipped on the overhead light so that he could read the map.

A small area to the east of Bandar Ma'Shur had been circled. Looking closer, Carter could see that what appeared to be a road had been penciled in on the map.

He looked up, then back at the map as he oriented himself.

The road would lead off this highway, perhaps ten miles farther to the east. It ran north from there at least fifteen miles inland, maybe as much as twenty. It was hard to tell from the map. But nothing else had been penciled in. The road inland ran to nothing. It was as if a stray pencil mark had been made on the map. But Carter was certain it wasn't a stray mark. Whatever had brought Lassiter and the short, squat man to Iran was there at the end of the pencil mark.

Zero-hour Strike Force?

He put the car in gear, made a U-turn on the highway, and headed east, driving slowly, watching for the turnoff as he neared the ten-mile mark.

There were a lot of oil rigs dotting the horizon inland, and not too far to the west was the major port city of Abadan. But here on the highway, with the Gulf to one side and the desert to the other, Carter could think for the time that he was utterly alone.

If it proved that his own government were involved with the nuclear strike on the Saudi oil fields, he wondered what his position would become. It would be impossible for him to continue. He was not one to shout "No nukes." If it came to war—necessary war for defense—he'd be the first in line to push the button. But a senseless nuclear strike against a friendly nation? The strike had served no other purpose than to embroil an already tense region of the world into a spiral of diplomatic threats and counterthreats and war preparations.

A little more than eleven miles from Bandar Ma'Shur he came to a turnoff prominently marked by a large billboard lit by bright lights. BANDAR MA'SHUR OIL RESEARCH COMPANY REGION SEVEN STATION. OIL RESEARCH TODAY FOR AN ENERGY-EFFICIENT TOMORROW.

He turned off the main road, then doused his lights as he headed out into the desert. What exactly was it he was expecting to find?

He clamped that thought off in his mind as he continued into the desert.

Soon what few lights he had seen to the west atop the oil pumping stations disappeared from view, and finally there was only the desert and the soft green glow of the car's dash lights.

As he drove, he thought for a while about Joy Makepiece back in Riyadh. He hoped that everything had turned out all right for the American peace delegation, but he had his doubts. With men like Lassiter and the short one running around so openly, it was a wonder this entire business hadn't been broken wide open by now. Had the Saudis gotten wind that the nuclear strike had possibly been an American action? God only knew what would happen if that ever came out. He shuddered even thinking about it.

There would be war. Of that he was certain.

The Region Seven oil research station turned out to consist of a number of huge corrugated metal Quonset huts dotted across a wide, flat section of the desert. There was a tall wire-mesh fence surrounding the entire area, but the gates were open, and there were no lights anywhere.

Carter slowly drove through the gates and along what had apparently served as the installation's main road. It was obvious that the dirt road had carried some very heavy traffic. In front of one of the larger buildings he could even pick out the marks of a half-track vehicle. Very likely more than one of them.

He pulled up and parked in front of one of the smaller huts, and got out of the car. He walked up the road for about fifty yards, then stopped and held his breath, listening. But there was nothing. Absolutely no sound. This far from the car there wasn't even the sound of the engine cooling. He turned slowly in a full circle. Only the buildings were there, silent and mute, except to the northwest where there was a curious flat openness.

He walked back to where the car was parked, but instead of getting into it, he went over to the hut and tried the door. It was open. Inside, he tried the light switch, but there was no electricity, which is what he suspected.

The building was empty. There was nothing here. No desks, no file cabinets, nothing. Not even a scrap of paper littering the floor.

Whoever had cleaned the place out had done an efficient job of it. Yet the building did not have the smell or the look of a place that had been *long* deserted. It had been occupied recently. There was that faint smell—or rather the combination of faint odors—that bespoke human habitation recently: food, office equipment, cleaning fluid, starch.

He turned and went back outside. He crossed the road and walked the hundred feet or so to the larger building, letting himself in through the wide service doors—wide enough, he supposed, to admit a large truck or tank.

This building was just as empty as the other, except at the far end he found a long, wide workbench, and on the floor, in four distinct areas, there were oil and grease stains. Something had been parked in here. Some four machines had been stored in here, and they had leaked their oil and had sweat grease on hot days.

Here the odors of recent occupation were much stronger; here Carter could smell the oil and the grease, and he could smell diesel fuel and even the faint odor of exhaust.

How long ago had it been since they had been here? he wondered. Certainly not months. Perhaps only days.

He returned to the car, drove down the road a hundred yards, jumped out, and hurried into one of the other buildings.

This one apparently had been a barracks. He could still see the marks the feet of the bunks had made on the floor, and spaced at regular intervals between each of the windows on both sides of the building were little alcoves with shelves for equipment and short bars on which to hang clothing.

Back outside, he jumped in the car again and quickly made a wide circuit of the camp, stopping in front of the various buildings and going in. But there was nothing. The camp had been cleaned out with the efficiency of a mother cleaning out a son's room after he had left for school.

What was this place? he asked himself back at the car. As before, he held his breath and listened to the eerie silence. Except this time he heard a faraway, deep-throated roar, which confused him for just a moment until he looked up. Far to the southwest—probably over the Gulf—were two tiny red dots, winking slowly on and off, moving toward the east. He connected the sound and the moving dots; they were a couple of high-flying jets. Probably military fighters on routine patrol over the Gulf. Possibly they were Iranian, perhaps even Iraqi. It was even possible, he had to concede, that they were American, although he didn't know if any of our carriers were based in the Gulf.

He slipped in behind the wheel and, with the window down, carefully drove out of the camp toward the open area to the northwest.

Beyond the last Quonset hut Carter suddenly bumped up onto a long, very wide slab of concrete.

The paved area had to be more than a hundred feet wide and possibly a mile long. Painted lines ran the length of the slab, right down the middle. A runway.

He lined the Mercedes up with the center marker and flipped on the headlights.

There were skid marks, long and black on the light concrete. Planes had taken off and landed here. Big planes. C-130s?

In the distance, near the far end of the runway, Carter could make out the darker outline of a long, low building. He put the car in gear and headed that way.

There was nothing here. At least nothing that he could use for proof or even a lead. This had obviously been some sort of a hastily built base—hasty, that is, except for the runway—that had been used for a time and had been recently abandoned.

The long, low building turned out to be a makeshift hangar with corrugated metal walls against the prevailing winds but only camouflage netting over the top. The netting was draped like a series of huge circus tents: four huge circus tents.

Carter drove off the runway, down a wide taxiway, and into the crude shelter. Slowly he made his way, by car, from one section of the flapping structure to the next, coming at last into the rear section where in a far corner was a pile of debris.

He headed directly for it, the headlights of the car shining on the pile of newspapers, magazines, hunks of metal, wood, and other junk.

A few feet away he stopped the car, and leaving the engine running and the lights on, he got out and approached the pile.

The first newspaper page he pulled out of the heap was from the English-language Paris edition of the *Herald-Tribune*, but the second was from a newspaper printed in Tel Aviv. In Hebrew.

He began digging through the pile in earnest, and all he found was junk: pieces of metal, twisted and bent beyond recognition; sections of the camouflage netting; bits of nylon rope, wire, and twine; and ordinary dirt and cement dust.

But then he found the automatic weapon clip.

At first he did not know what he had found. He felt the long smooth object beneath a piece of cardboard. But when he brought it out into the bright illumination of the headlights he recognized it immediately.

Stamped on the lower left-hand corner of the case was the

word Uzi. It was an empty clip for the Israeli-built Uzi submachine gun.

For a long time he stood there looking at the clip. Uzi. The planes that had apparently delivered the nuclear weapons to the Saudi oil field had been marked with the Star of David.

There was a connection, albeit tenuous, between that event and what he had found here. But it was a connection nevertheless.

He turned and looked back down the long, angled column of shelters. The concrete floor was thick, as thick as the runway. These four shelter areas could easily have held Hercules aircraft.

He went back to the car and got in, his mind seething. He tossed the Uzi ammunition clip on the passenger seat, swung the car around in a wide looping arc, and slowly headed toward the front exit. Only this time he kept his eyes searching the concrete floor.

Off to the right side of the front building he found what he was afraid he might.

He stopped the car and got out again, approaching the far edge of the concrete floor. In several spots on the floor there were faint traces of blue and white paint.

He stared at the paint mists; overspraying. Blue for the Star of David, white for the trim.

It was clear. But if they had painted the Star of David on the aircraft here, what markings had the planes come in with?

He took out his handkerchief and laid it on the floor next to a particularly thick section of paint mist. Then he pulled out his penknife and scraped a bit of the blue and some of the white off the floor, depositing the tiny chips in his handkerchief, which he folded and put in his pocket.

He went back to the car, got in, and drove out onto the runway and headed back to the camp.

Everything pointed to the likelihood that American C-130

Hercules aircraft had somehow been brought here to this base in Iran. That in itself was an amazing accomplishment considering the strained relationship between the two countries. Then the Israeli markings had been painted on the airplanes, which took off from the long airstrip and delivered the bombs to the Saudi oil fields.

Carter had to admit that it was all circumstantial evidence. Very strong evidence, but circumstantial nevertheless.

At the end of the runway, he turned down the dirt road that led through the camp and headed toward the front gate. He glanced over at the Uzi ammunition clip and shook his head. He lit a cigarette.

Somehow he was going to have to get down to Al Kuwait. From there he could take a commercial flight back to . . .

He stopped cold. Back to where? Washington, where he'd present the ammunition clip and the paint chips to Hawk? Afterward would he tender his resignation?

"So what do you make of this, Nick?" Hawk would ask.

"Sir?"

"You've brought me back paint chips and a clip that I could have bought within five minutes of this office. So what? What have you found? *That's* what I'm asking you!"

What the hell *had* he found? Nothing.

The doorways and windows of the Quonset huts he passed seemed like malevolent eyes, accusing and staring. There was nothing here. Or at least nothing conclusive.

As far as he could see, the evidence pointed two ways. The first, and most obvious to him, was toward his own country. Toward his own government. But the other was toward Israel. The surface evidence was toward Jerusalem.

He slowed down at the main gate and looked in the rearview mirror at the silhouettes of the dark buildings. What had happened here? Certainly this had been more than an oil research station.

What *had* happened here?

It was well after 4:00 A.M. by the time Carter made it back to the main road. Al Kuwait was about 150 miles to the southwest. Over the water it was a straight shot, but by land it was an impossible trip. A twenty-five-mile-wide strip of Iraq lay between Iran and the relative safety of Kuwait.

By land or by sea? By sea it would probably be safe. But supposing he could find a boat, even a fast boat that might do twelve or fifteen knots—it would still take him eight to ten hours for the trip. Eight to ten precious hours. Overland there would be trouble: first from the Iranians; then from the Iraqis; and finally from the Kuwaitis, who did not take kindly to people crashing their borders. But it would be a very fast trip. At the inside he might make it in as little as a couple of hours. At the outside, with luck, three or four hours.

He looked at his watch; it was 4:30. Unless he was detained—or worse—he could conceivably make it to Al Kuwait by 6:30 or 7:30. At the latest, he would be in plenty of time for the early morning flights to . . .

Where? he had to ask himself again. Washington, D.C., or . . . Tel Aviv?

He knew the answer. He would not return from the Middle East until he had the answer or until he knew that he could not, under any circumstances, find the answer here.

There was nothing out on the highway. Absolutely nothing as he turned west, skirting Bandar Ma'Shur, then speeding up, the big Mercedes flying down the highway.

At times, driving, Carter felt as if he were running away from a demon back at the base. But the faster and more recklessly he drove, mindless now of his wounds, which were once again beginning to bother him, the closer the demon seemed to come.

He had spent most of his adult life in service to his country.

And now he was faced with a huge personal crisis. What would he do if it proved that the U.S. had attacked Saudi Arabia with nuclear weapons? What in God's name would he do?

He burst through the town of Shahdegan, thirty-five miles west of Bandar Ma'Shur, doing just under ninety. There were a few buildings on the outskirts of the town of six thousand, then a concentration of buildings and a couple of trucks, all moving past in a blur, then the heart of the oil town, and once again he was out on the open highway, a flashing blue light dropping well back behind him.

On both sides of the highway the land had flattened out, and a thick, lush, junglelike forest grew toward the interior. The Biblical land of Eden.

He stopped about twenty-five miles southwest of Shahdegan and switched on the interior light so he could read the map.

Abadan was a few miles to the west and the north now, and the border with Iraq was just a few miles almost due west. At this point he would have to cross the border, then race through twenty-five miles of the countryside to the border town of Umm Qasr. From there it was less than two miles to the Kuwaiti frontier and then the long run to Al Kuwait itself.

He took out the .357 and checked to make sure it was ready to fire. He cranked up the passenger side window and cranked down his window, then slipped the car in gear and accelerated down the highway toward whatever. . . .

TWELVE

The highway dipped down and down closer to the Persian Gulf as it approached the delta bridge over the combined Tigris and Euphrates rivers, which was the border between Iran and Iraq.

There had not been much fighting here; most of it was confined to the desert areas of the far north. But there were military emplacements on either side of the road, far off the highway, the antiaircraft guns and rocket platforms silhouetted in the early morning darkness.

Carter was certain that by now his movement toward the border had been noted. It wouldn't be long before he'd be challenged and then, ultimately, fired upon. He only hoped that his sudden intrusion, the fact that he was driving a civilian vehicle, and his high rate of speed would serve to shock the Iranian forces into inaction long enough for him to cross the border into Iraq. What the Iraqis might do was an entirely different story.

Carter happened to look up and to the west in time to see several intense flashes of light. For a long time afterward there was nothing, but then the dull explosions came in on the night air.

They were Iranian or Iraqi interceptor-fighters battling in the night sky.

He heard the distant roar of the jets, and then there was another series of intensely bright flashes, these much closer, the thunder coming much faster.

A pair of high-performance military jets screamed overhead from east to west—Iranian—releasing four rocket trails. They were air-to-air missiles, Carter realized. At that moment a bright flash came just above him, followed almost simultaneously by the roar of a tremendous explosion that lit up the countryside and rolled across the hills. Debris began falling out of the sky to the northwest like shooting stars. Another flash lit up the sky far to the west as another of the Iranian air-to-air rockets found its mark.

Suddenly Carter saw the bridge approach down a long stretch of highway. Sandbags lined both sides of the road, and at one point he was able to pick out four soldiers manning a mobile radar installation on the back of a large truck.

But then he flashed by them doing in excess of a hundred miles per hour.

He had to concentrate on his driving. The road at this point was not very good. Debris littered the surface, and once he had to swerve to avoid a very large bomb crater.

They began shooting at him from the Iranian side when he was less than a mile from the bridge. A large steel barrier was lowered across the road, and as he pressed harder on the accelerator, heavy-caliber bullets penetrated the body of the car. He looked on both sides of the road for a way around the obstacle, but there was nothing. To the inland side were sandbags piled very high, and on the seaward side was a ten-foot drop to the Gulf.

He had started to brake when the barrier slowly began to rise. For just a moment he could not believe what he was seeing. The steel border-crossing barrier was actually coming up.

He could see the Iraqi soldiers at the border post by the flashes of their automatic weapons. At first he thought they were shooting at him, but when he was just about on top of the post he understood that they were answering the fire from the Iranians that had been directed at Carter.

But then he was on the bridge, accelerating again, well past the hundred-sixty-kilometers-per-hour mark on the speedometer, up to the center span, a lurch when he hit the top, then down the other side, the road curving ever so gently to the south as it looped through farm fields intermingled with oil rigs.

He looked in his rearview mirror. There were a lot of flashes from behind, from the other side of the bridge. There would be fighting probably until dawn. Maybe longer. But by some unspoken, unwritten agreement, the bridge itself had never been seriously damaged. Both sides realized that the war would be over sooner or later. And when it was, they'd need the bridge. The oil companies would need the bridge. No one was willing to knock it down.

There were no towns or villages between the border with Iran and the border with Kuwait, except for Umm Qasr, which was right on the narrow bay that separated Iraq from her neighbor to the south. He made very good time, crossing the twenty-five-mile stretch of land in just over fifteen minutes.

He slowed down as he approached the town, passed through it, and on the other side slipped the magnum beneath his seat and stopped at the border crossing.

The Iraqi border guard came out of his post, yawning. There was no trouble here. Kuwait and Iraq were on friendly terms. But the man's eyes widened when he saw the bullet holes in the Mercedes. The Kuwaiti border guard had come out of his post, and he ducked beneath the barrier pole and walked across.

Carter got out of the car shaking his head. He pulled out his

French passport and handed it to the Iraqi. "Marcel Mentoir," he said.

"What has happened here, Monsieur Mentoir?" the Kuwaiti asked.

"I was in Abadan, and those crazy bastard Iranians tried to kill me."

The Iraqi guard stiffened at the mention of the Iranian city. "What were you doing there, monsieur, in an enemy country?" He had his hand on the butt of his pistol.

"Trying to sell those fools oil pumping equipment."

"And did you?"

Again Carter shook his head and shrugged. "I . . ." He hesitated, appealing to the two men with his gestures. "It was an affair of the heart, I am afraid."

"The heart . . ." the Iraqi started, not understanding, but then he realized what Carter meant. "And they shot at you?"

"They came after me, so I felt the safest place for me would be here. When I was coming across the border, the fools really opened up. But your border people opened the barrier for me."

The Iraqi looked at him for a long moment, then turned to the Kuwaiti. They conferred for a moment or two in Arabic, and then they turned back to Carter.

"What is it you wish to do here, Monsieur Mentoir?" the Iraqi asked.

"Cross into Kuwait."

The Kuwaiti spoke up. "And in my country?"

"I wish only to drive to Al Kuwait, where I will drop this automobile off for repair and then take the first flight to Cairo."

"I see," the Kuwaiti said. "Then you will offer no objections if I search your car?"

"None," Carter said, "but I will tell you now I have a weapon. It is a pistol beneath the front seat." He didn't tell them about the other gun, the .38 Police Special he had gotten from the short man in the Sheraton parking lot. He hoped that if the border guards found one, they might search no further. Although, he told himself, it didn't really matter if he were armed or not from this point on. He would not be able to take the weapons with him aboard the commercial flight to Cairo.

The Kuwaiti stepped back while the Iraqi guard walked past Carter and fished under the seat for the gun, coming up with the magnum. He brought out the gun with a lot of respect on his face.

"This is a very large gun, monsieur," he said.

"One I have not used. In fact it is not mine. I took it from the man who tried to kill me with it."

"Then you will have no objections to us keeping this here," the Iraqi said.

"None."

"We have no wish for such a weapon to enter our country," the Kuwaiti guard said.

"I understand."

The Kuwaiti took Carter's passport and went back across the border into his post. He was gone only a moment or two, and when he came back he returned Carter's passport. "I have stamped this only for passage. You must be out of Kuwait within twenty-four hours. Do you understand, monsieur?"

"I understand. *Merci.*"

He climbed into the Mercedes, started it, and headed across the border as the barrier post was raised.

"*Au revoir*," he said, accelerating.

It was just a minute or two after 7:00 when Carter came into the city of Al Kuwait. He parked his car in the long-term parking area at the airport and went into the terminal. The next flight to Cairo was loading at that moment.

His passport was in order and he had no luggage, so he was able to purchase his ticket and board the aircraft with no trouble at all.

They were airborne fifteen minutes later. The flight attendants served coffee, and Carter sat back with his and lit a cigarette.

From Cairo he planned on flying to Cyprus and taking the shuttle from there to Tel Aviv. While in Cyprus, however, he'd telephone Hawk to find out about Kimi Móudhros and about his weapons. He had a bad feeling about that, but there was absolutely nothing he could do until he contacted Hawk.

He hoped that something could be set up for him in Tel Aviv. If not, his only option, he figured, would be to find out if there were any active American bases within Israel. Local CIA operations would have come up with something like that if it were the case.

Once again Carter had a tough time forcing himself to think this out, to think that the Zero-hour Strike Force was an American-sponsored nuclear unit.

They landed in Cairo at 9:30 A.M. local time, and Carter wasn't able to get a flight out to Cyprus until 11:00, landing in Nicosia an hour and a half later. He booked himself on the 4:00 flight to Tel Aviv, then took a cab into town to the telephone exchange.

It was a pleasant, warm, sunny day, and even if this respite was only temporary, it felt good for the moment. His call to David Hawk at AXE headquarters on Dupont Circle went through without delay. It was very early in the morning in Washington, but Hawk was already at his desk.

"Nicholas," Hawk said. "We were happy to hear that you are in Nicosia. We've been worried since you left Athens."

"What about Kimi, sir?" Carter asked.

"Dead," Hawk said guardedly. "One of the people responsible died in the escape attempt, but your package has been secured."

Kimi dead! Christ, they had been on him from the start.

"Where shall we send your things?"

"Tel Aviv."

"The embassy—" Hawk started, but Carter cut him off.

"No, sir. Not there."

"Are you trying to tell me something, N3?"

"Yes, sir," Carter said. He pulled Lassiter's ID out, and read the name, address, and ID number to Hawk. The details were being recorded. "Send my things to the chief of station for the Company in Tel Aviv. For-your-eyes-only designation for me."

"I see," Hawk said. "Do you need anything else?"

"Clothing, a suitcase, that sort of stuff, sir. My replacements were left on the doorstep of the French embassy in Tehran." In very guarded terms, Carter told Hawk everything that had happened to him since he had left Kimitri Móudhros. "I'm leaving for Tel Aviv in a couple of hours. I'll stay at the Dan Hotel until my things catch up with me."

"We can have everything over to you within a few hours. It'll be there very soon after you," Hawk assured him. "And I have a pleasant surprise for you."

"Sir?"

"Our people were released, unharmed, from the hotel in Riyadh."

"Do you know if a woman by the name of Joy Makepiece was included in those released?"

"No," Hawk said. "But I can find out for you."

"You might check into it, sir. If she wasn't released, perhaps we should make some waves."

"Will do. We're also checking into this other thing that was referred to in our files, but then removed."

"Anything yet, sir?"

"I'm afraid not. But we're working on it. Take care, Nicholas."

"Yes, sir."

Carter hung up, then went to the counter and paid for the call. Back outside he stopped at a small restaurant for lunch, finally making it back to the airport around three, where he bought a Paris *Herald-Tribune* and a pack of cigarettes. He missed his own brand, which were made up specially for him by a small shop in Washington.

He checked in with El Al, got his boarding pass, then went into the waiting area where he sat back.

Front-page headlines screamed about the war threats over the Middle East oil fields. Israel, the newspaper reported, had become an armed camp.

There had been a fresh wave of fighting all across the Iran-Iraq border.

The government of Saudi Arabia apologized to the Swiss Red Cross for kicking them out of the country. The Saudis also apologized profusely to the American peace talks delegation and to the staff of the embassy in Riyadh for the recent misunderstanding.

War hysteria was building across the Middle East.

And in the U.S. the slogan *Save Our Oil* was on everyone's lips.

His flight was announced. He laid the newspaper aside, stubbed out his cigarette, and boarded with the other passengers who were waiting. No one seemed happy. No one seemed expectant. These were difficult times.

It was only 250 miles southwest to Tel Aviv, so it was just a little before five when they set down at Lod Airport. The airfield was bristling with military activity. Jets screamed down the parallel runway for takeoffs; armored vehicles, jeeps, troop trucks, and even tanks seemed to be parked everywhere. Israel was a nation ready for war.

Carter's papers were scrutinized with special care, and it wasn't until six before he was cleared through and was able to catch a cab for the long drive into the city.

The cabby was a taciturn older man who either didn't like Carter because he was a foreigner or because as an able-bodied man he wasn't in uniform. Either way it was a quiet ride into the city. Carter would have liked it otherwise. Often, on assignments like this, he could pick up the flavor of the city he was coming into—pick up a feel for the mood of the people and of the government—from a talkative taxi driver.

Just as in Saudi Arabia, and in Iran and Iraq, the roadsides in many spots were used for mobile radar units, antiaircraft rocket installations, and other gun emplacements.

At the Dan, a nice hotel right on the Mediterranean just off the downtown section of the city, Carter was given a pleasant room overlooking the sea. The people here, like those throughout the city, were distant and preoccupied. At any moment war could erupt, and this time it would most likely escalate into a full-fledged nuclear confrontation.

From room service he ordered a light supper, a bottle of cognac, and the local English-language newspaper. While he was waiting for his meal to come up, he stripped off his clothes and climbed into a steaming hot shower. Later, he turned off the hot water and forced himself to remain under the cold spray for a full five minutes.

His bandages were soaked through. When he stepped out of the shower he was leaking blood. He pressed a towel against his shoulder wound and wrapped another around his waist, then padded into his room where he dialed the front desk and asked for the house doctor to be sent up.

"I was injured several days ago, and I'm afraid I've opened the wound. It's not too serious, but I'd like it attended to."

"Of course, Monsieur Mentoir," the desk clerk said solicitously.

Five minutes later his dinner—corned beef, rye bread, and

a selection of cheeses and pickles—and the cognac arrived. A few minutes after that the doctor showed up.

He was a very old man with wild white hair, reminding Carter of Einstein. He made Carter sit on a chair in the bathroom, and he disinfected the wound and put a couple of stitches in it.

"When were you shot, monsieur?" the doctor asked in French.

"A couple of days ago in Tehran," Carter replied. "They are all crazy over there."

The doctor looked at him, an indulgent smile on his lips. "Indeed," he said. "And what were you doing in Tehran?"

"Selling oil pumping equipment . . . *trying* to sell my products, that is. And without much success, I might add."

"I can see that."

Someone knocked at the door.

"Could you see to that, Doctor?" Carter asked.

The doctor went across the bedroom and opened the door. Joy Makepiece stood there, a large brown suitcase in her hand.

"Oh," she said, stepping back and looking at the room number.

Carter had gotten up. *"Ma chérie!"* he said. "It is I, Marcel!"

She picked up on it immediately. "Marcel," she cried, hurrying into the room. She dropped the suitcase in the middle of the room and raced across to him, clucking like a mother hen. "And what now, you have gone and had another accident?"

"I'm afraid it is more than that, *mon petit chon*," he said. "Some fool tried to kill me."

"No," she said. "Don't tell me—a jealous husband? Marcel!"

The doctor laughed. "If you will just wait, young lady, I

will have your young man as good as new . . . or nearly so. It will just be a few minutes."

Back in the bathroom, the doctor finished attending to Carter's wounds. then winked at him. "She is lovely. You are a very lucky man, monsieur."

"Thank you, Doctor," Carter said. "And yes, I believe you are correct—I am a very lucky man."

When the doctor left, Joy practically leaped on him. "What the hell happened to you?"

"What are you doing here?"

"Not fair," she said. "I asked first. What happened to you, and how did you get here?"

Carter had put the suitcase on the stand beside the dresser. He opened it. Inside were clothes as well as a new Pierre, Hugo, and Wilhelmina. He picked up the Luger and tested its action. It was perfect. He loaded it, then quickly checked the stiletto and gas bomb.

Joy got a couple of glasses from the bathroom and poured them each a drink. She handed Carter his, then perched on the edge of the writing desk. "Now, would you please tell me how you got out of Riyadh? Sutherland was very worried about you. And so was I. Not bad considering neither of us knows who the hell you are."

Carter sipped at his drink, then lit a cigarette. Quickly he told her nearly everything that had happened to him from the moment they had entered the hotel in Riyadh. He only left out his calls to David Hawk.

When he was finished, she just stared at him for a few long moments. Then she got up, poured them both another drink, and shook her head.

"A nifty story, Nick, but it doesn't add up. At just the crucial times, someone evidently tells you something. You have someone at your beck and call who evidently has a lot of pull. I mean one minute I'm dressed as a man and I'm sneaking out of the hotel in Riyadh, then I'm in Paris getting debriefed. Before I know it I'm aboard an American military jet with a brown suitcase in my hand, screaming at sixty thousand feet across the Med for this hotel. Lordy. You've got a lot of pull.''

Carter smiled. "And you must be the best. I asked for the chief of station to meet me here.''

She got an odd look. "You haven't heard?'' she asked.

He shook his head, a cold feeling coming over him.

"The chief of station for Central Intelligence Agency activities for the entire Middle East, including Israel, was assassinated this afternoon.''

THIRTEEN

"I was told the moment I landed," Joy said. "The assistant chief of station, Don Prescott, will be over here at ten o'clock tonight to brief you. He said he was waiting for some information to come in that he was to pass on to you."

Carter said nothing. They had expected him in Athens, and Tehran, and now here in Tel Aviv.

She looked at the weapons. "I was told to bring these things to you immediately."

Carter turned and went over to the window that looked out across the Mediterranean. There were times, such as this moment, when he wondered if anything he had ever done had accomplished a thing. Or had he been batting his head against the proverbial wall? Was it all some vast game in which the outcome never really mattered, and the only significant thing that ever happened was the death of one or more of the participants?

Many years ago one of his trainers at AXE had advised him that in this business there was always the risk of turning cynical.

Was that what was finally happening to him? After a hundred different operations? After hundreds of killings? His designation was N3 Killmaster. A license to kill. Not like in espionage adventure novels, but for real. Real guns. Real bullets. Real blood and screams and pleas for mercy.

Joy had come up behind him, and she gently placed a hand on his bare shoulder. He nearly jumped out of his skin. But he held back from turning around for just a moment. For the first time in his long, intense career, he was being challenged on a front he never dreamed he'd be forced to deal with: his own loyalty. America—love her or leave her. America—right or wrong.

Goddamnit, he thought. Was he being used to cover up his country's participation in some insane nuclear escapade? One way or the other—and it really did matter which way it fell—he would pursue this to its end. And if he had been crossed, if he had been lied to, used, manipulated . . . so help him God, there would be hell to pay.

He turned around to Joy, whose lips were parted and whose eyes were wide. She came easily into his arms, her lips warm and pliant, her eager body molding easily against his, her full breasts crushed against his chest.

He stroked her neck and she shivered. "I was worried about you," she said.

"You're not supposed to worry in this business."

They parted and she looked up into his eyes. "No, I mean it, Nick. In Riyadh you were like some kind of a masked man coming in on a white charger. I didn't know what was happening sometimes. One minute you were there, and the next minute all hell was breaking loose in the soccer stadium across from us, and then you were pulling me out of the hole."

"You came up with Kebir. He has been the key so far." He could still see the young man lying there in the sewer, could still hear those four words. *Zero-hour Strike Force.*

"Without your diversion, and your pulling me out of there, it wouldn't have made a damned bit of difference what we had learned."

She disengaged herself from his arms and went over to the bed where she stood a moment, then she pulled down the spread. She turned toward Carter and took off her clothes, item by item, until she stood there nude. He dropped the towel around his waist and came to her. Together they eased themselves onto the cool sheets.

Carter was in a very tender mood, and he treated her with a great gentleness, stroking her breasts, and her stomach, and her thighs for a long time. Kissing her neck, and her ears, and her full, sensuous lips.

She too was gentle, partially because she was concerned about his wounds, so obvious with the new bandages around his side and at his shoulder, and partially because she was frightened.

From what she had learned so far, and from what he had told her he had found, she had come to nearly the same conclusions he had. She was worried that her own country had done such a despicable act that she would never be able to live with it. Could she continue to work in defense of the U.S. if her wildest fears were true?

At one point she whimpered, and he propped himself up on one elbow and looked down at her. She opened her eyes, her lips parted, her breath coming in short gasps.

"What is it?" he asked softly.

She shook her head, her long blond hair fanning out over the pillow. Tears came to the corners of her eyes and leaked down the sides of her face.

"What is it?" he asked again.

"Nothing," she said. "Just love me, Nick . . . please, just love me."

She drew him closer, her legs spreading, and soon he entered her, and she responded in sync with his rhythm as if they had lived together for years.

She clung tightly to him, her arms around his neck, her legs around his waist, coming, coming with him, until she cried out sharply, her entire body shuddering, then arching in pleasure.

Don Prescott, the assistant chief of operations for the Middle East, turned out to be a bland-looking banker type, showing up at the stroke of ten in a natty three-piece suit and carrying a briefcase.

Carter and Joy had slept a little, had taken a shower together, shared the food Carter had ordered but hadn't had a chance to eat, and had a couple of drinks. When Prescott showed up they were ready for him.

"Mr. Carter," Prescott said, his voice pinched. He was a slight man in his mid-fifties with curly gray hair.

"I was told that your boss was assassinated this afternoon."

"Yes, sir," the man said. "It was a bomb. Plastique, we think, beneath the driver's seat of his car, and again beneath the gasoline tank. There was no possibility of survival."

"What kind of a fuse?"

"Almost certainly radio controlled."

"Then it was someone new to the scene. Someone who hadn't the time to establish his routine. They took the risk of detection so that they would be certain to get to him."

"Yes, sir," Prescott said. He was not enjoying this.

"Why?" Carter asked.

"Sir?"

"Why kill him now? Was he on to something?"

"Well," Prescott said, suddenly very businesslike. "Well. I've come for the matter of briefing you. The DCA himself messaged us."

"But he didn't mention being totally honest and open with me."

"Presumably you have queried U.S. involvement in Israeli defense installations—"

"Listen, Don, all I want to know is if there are any American military bases presently maintained on Israeli soil. Not too difficult a request to comprehend."

Prescott ignored the sarcasm. "There was one base that was out near the Dead Sea. Forty or forty-five miles south-west of here, near the very small town of Mār Sābā. It's an ancient village, there are certain religious ruins that—"

"A base *was* out there? Past tense?" Carter asked impatiently.

"That's right. We believe there was a training center. Army Airborne. Green Berets. That sort of thing."

"But it has been closed?"

"We think so, but we're not a hundred percent sure."

"How long ago do your people suspect it may have closed?" Carter asked.

"I don't know for sure."

"Years, months, weeks?"

"Certainly not years or even months."

"Weeks?"

Prescott shrugged. "Perhaps days. We're just not sure."

" 'Perhaps days,' " Carter repeated, looking incredulously at the man. There had been a nuclear strike on a friendly nation, and within days of that event, a secret American military installation on Israeli soil had perhaps, or perhaps not, been closed down. He glanced over at Joy, and she too was flabbergasted.

"Prescott, your days here in the Middle East have just come to a close," Carter said. "I want you to get your ass out of here and pack. Within a few days you'll be receiving orders, reassigning you home. Now get the hell out of my sight."

Prescott looked from Joy to Carter and back to Joy again. "All right then," he said. "Ms. Makepiece, you *will* come with me."

"No, sir," Joy said firmly. "I'll stay with Mr. Carter. There is a lot of work to do."

"You're fired," he said.

Joy laughed, and Prescott turned and left the room. Carter whistled long and low. "What about him? Have you heard anything about the man?"

"Not a thing," she said. "What an asshole."

Carter had to laugh. "I couldn't have picked a better word myself. How did he get this far . . .?" He thought for a moment, then looked into her eyes. "I'd advise you to cut out now, for your own good."

"No," she said instantly.

"I was hoping you'd say that. Well, we'd better get to work. I want you to find us a car. The sturdier the better. And get us some detailed maps of the country."

"Will do," she said. "One hour, in the lobby?"

"Let's make it the back entrance."

Joy started to leave, but Carter stopped her. "Once you get the car, don't leave it. Not even for a moment or two."

She nodded grimly and then was gone.

Carter waited five minutes, then he too left the room and took the elevator to the first floor. From there he found the rear stairwell, which he took to the ground floor. He skirted the lobby, entered the dining room, and left the hotel by the side exit. He walked around to the front and got a cab.

"The American trade mission," Carter told the driver.

The man turned around. "Never heard of it."

"It's off Sderot David Hamelech, near the WIZO-Child Center."

"Yes, sir," he said, and they took off.

It took only five minutes to drive into the downtown section of the city, where Carter got out at a squat, red brick building that looked more like it belonged off the Boston Common than here in Israel.

He paid the cab and went into the narrow entryway, then down a dark corridor to a Dutch door, the top half of which was open. Beyond was a desk at which sat a young man of about twenty-five. He jumped up when Carter appeared.

"May I help you, sir?"

"I want to speak with the OD," Carter said softly. "Yellow six-six-six."

"Yellow, six . . ." the young man started, but then his mouth opened and no sound came out for a moment. "Oh . . . my . . . gosh," he managed to stammer, and he went back to his desk and got on the phone. "George," he said, "we have a triple sixes—a yellow!"

He put the phone down, and literally a second or two later an older, gray-haired man came out. "Mr. Carter?" he asked.

"You were told I'd be coming?"

"Of course, sir," the man said, and he let Carter inside. They went down a corridor to a small office furnished only with a desk, a couple of file cabinets, and a map of Israel. The American trade mission in any country is usually used as the clearinghouse for intelligence activities in that country, especially if it's a friendly country. Most field agents are unaware of this. Usually only one or two top people in each intelligence unit know the extent of the collation and coordination work the trade missions do. But that was all the trade mission did. It never fielded agents, it made no analysis or judgment of anything fed to it. It merely collated and assembled whatever data came its way, digested it, and made sure it got to the proper end users by an alternate channel from that used by the intelligence units it supplemented.

"What can I do for you, Mr. Carter?"

"Don Prescott?"

"Not a nice man, but harmless. He's advanced as far as he'll ever advance."

"Joy Makepiece?"

"Not familiar with the name. Should I be?"

"An American military advisory installation near the town of Mār Sābā?"

The OD looked oddly at him. "I'm sorry, Mr. Carter, that's one bit of gossip I'm afraid I don't know a thing about."

Carter got up from where he had been sitting. "Any American installations here in Israel?"

"Weather stations, consulates, trade missions, and the like?"

"Military."

The man shook his head. "Sorry, sir. And I mean that in all honesty."

"Sure," Carter said, sick at heart. He turned and left the office, letting himself out.

Two blocks later he caught a cab back to the Dan. All the way there he kept watching out the back window, expecting at any moment to pick up a tail. But he remained clean, pulling into the front driveway of the hotel a couple of minutes before eleven.

He paid the cabby and went up to his room, where he set up several intrusion indicators. Then he called down to the desk, leaving a wakeup call for 8:00 A.M.

When he was finished, he let himself out of the room—leaving the door unbugged to give whoever might try to get in a false sense of security—and took the back stairs all the way down to the ground floor, where he slipped out the back exit onto the hotel's loading dock.

Joy hadn't shown up yet, but it was still a few minutes early. He lit a cigarette and, cupping the lit end with his hand, stepped back into the shadows to wait.

Prescott had known of the Mār Sābā American base, but the trade mission had not. One of them had lied or was lying.

Either Prescott and the CIA installation here in Tel Aviv had not told the entire truth to the trade mission, or the mission specialist had lied tonight to Carter. It didn't really matter which, although either way it was disturbing.

Headlights flashed from around the corner at the far end of the parking lot. A moment later a Land-Rover pulled up at the loading dock, and Joy Makepiece got out.

"Nick?" she called softly.

Carter remained standing in the shadows, watching the direction she had come from, scanning the cars and trucks in the lot. But there was nothing. No one had followed her; no one was watching her.

He stepped out of the shadows. "Oh, there you are," she said. "I didn't think you had come down yet."

Carter jumped down off the loading dock and got in on the passenger side. Joy climbed back in behind the wheel.

"I did some checking," he told her. "No one has heard of any American military base in Israel."

"Why would Prescott make up such a story?"

"I don't think he did."

"Then . . . whoever you spoke with was either not very well informed—or not telling the truth."

He nodded. "Did you get a map?"

"Yes. Let's go." She pulled out of the parking lot, drove around to the front of the hotel, then across town to Ramat Hatayasim where she picked up the main highway that ran southwest past Lod Airport and eventually to Jerusalem, where they could pick up the road that led out into the desert to the town of Mār Sābā.

It was after midnight before they cleared the city and she was able to speed up, but then they made good time. The road twisted through the ancient hills, the cedar trees silhouetted against the horizon, but there was little traffic.

Out here at night, Carter could feel the sense of history.

This had been among the first places where civilization flourished. It very well could be, he thought morosely, where civilization ended.

They made the thirty miles to the Israeli capital city in about forty-five minutes. They skirted the downtown area and within fifteen minutes were bumping along a narrow secondary road toward Mār Sābā.

This was suddenly very reminiscent of his experience earlier that day in southern Iran, tracking down another base. He wondered if he'd find this one, and if it too would be as cleaned out as the other one.

A half hour later they came to the village of Mār Sābā, which consisted only of a tiny, ancient church and a half-dozen crude buildings. There were no lights and no movement as they drove down its single street and out the other side.

The road only ran another few miles before it finally petered out. But Carter could see where half-track vehicles had come this way before.

Joy slipped the Land-Rover into four-wheel drive, and they pushed on, Carter scanning the horizon in every direction.

But it wasn't necessary; the tracks led a few miles farther to a fenced-in area that contained a dozen Quonset huts, some of them quite large, and in the distance they could see a long runway. This base was almost the exact duplicate of the one in Iran.

The front gate was open, so they drove through and down a row of long buildings, pulling up in front of one of the larger structures. Joy killed the Land-Rover's engine.

"We're going to take the buildings one by one," Carter said. "Look for anything, anything at all, that might tell us something."

"They're abandoned."

"That's right, but something might have been left behind," Carter said, and he hopped out of the car. "You take the one across the street. I'll try the big one."

Joy hurried across the dirt road and disappeared into one of the buildings. Carter turned and slipped inside the larger building, whose large service doors had probably admitted some kind of vehicles. He left the doors open so that he could use what little starlight there was.

They had been in more of a hurry clearing out this base. There were a lot of tools and equipment lying around. A file cabinet sat in one corner, all its drawers open. It was cleaned out, as was a tall cabinet that had once held books.

He turned around slowly, studying the maintenance shed. Books, he thought. Maintenance manuals. There would be several of them for the half-track vehicles. But they would need stacks of them for the C-130 Hercules aircraft.

He hurried back out to the car and beeped the horn a couple of times. Joy came out of the building in a dead run.

"What happened?" she shouted.

"Get in," Carter said. He climbed behind the wheel and took off the moment she sat down.

"Where are we going? What's happening?"

Carter drove straight through the camp and out to the runway. The layout was the same as in Iran. There were a series of four large shelters at the far end of the runway. Shelters big enough for the C-130s.

"Maintenance manuals," Carter shouted breathlessly. Whoever it was had been in a hurry when they cleared out of here. There was debris all over the place. They had worked on the half-tracks; no doubt they had also worked on the C-130s. Maybe, just maybe, they had overlooked one maintenance manual. Just one somewhere in the junk.

Carter explained all that to her in quick, clipped sentences, and by the time they drove into the aircraft shelters, Joy was ready for the search.

There was junk everywhere. Construction debris, empty

oil cans, broken tools, worn-out parts.

Joy found the master hydraulic system manual for the Hercules C-130. It had fallen behind one of the cabinets that contained cans of hydraulic fluid.

Carter took the book back to the Land-Rover, flipped on the headlights, and opened the book to the letter of promulgation found in every military manual.

"Shit," he said, looking at the letterhead. It was the final proof.

"What is it?" Joy asked. Carter held the book out so she could see the letterhead.

Davis-Monthan Air Force Base, Tucson, Arizona.

FOURTEEN

They took the early morning flight to Paris, and from there the connecting flight to New York. The trip took fourteen hours, but with the eight-hour difference in time zones, they landed at Kennedy at one that afternoon.

From the moment they had left Tel Aviv, and during their ground time at Orly outside Paris and again in New York, Carter had the distinct impression that they were being followed. He wasn't certain, but he felt the itchy tingle between his shoulder blades.

Joy managed to get a little sleep on the plane, but Carter's mind had been alive with conjecture and, he had to admit, a certain feeling of betrayal. Now that it seemed certain that the U.S. had engineered and pulled off the nuclear strike against the Saudi oil fields, he found that he felt like a tight-rope walker whose net had just been taken away. Carter was a product of the States. He had defended her, fought for her, and laid his life on the line for her interests for so long that the thought of his government having done something so despicable was unsettling.

When Joy woke up, about two hours out of New York, they had spoken about it. She had the same feelings as Carter:

a sense of not belonging, that the props had been knocked out from under her.

An even bigger blow came, however, when they got off the plane in New York and walked into the terminal. All incoming flights from Israel were being picketed.

> GO HOME!
> DEATH TO ZIONISTS!
> SAVE OUR OIL!

There were several hundred demonstrators, many of them carrying signs, some of them chanting the popular "Save Our Oil" slogan.

Carter and Joy made their way through customs. Carter now used his original passport; his weapons had been sealed in a diplomatic bag that had been arranged for him in Paris. Soon they were in the main terminal, and Carter went into a men's room, where he unsealed the bag, pulled out his weapons, and strapped them on, one by one.

Carter and Joy had decided that they were going to see this thing through to the end. Carter could be certain about Hawk, but Joy could not be certain about her chain of command, so she agreed to tag along with him rather than work through Langley. Carter had also decided that whatever they found—no matter how bad—was going to be acted upon.

When he had said that, Joy had looked at him round-eyed, and she asked him exactly what he meant by it.

"I'll stop whoever started it," he said.

"If the President ordered it?"

"I'll kill him," Carter said grimly.

Now, looking at his reflection in the rest room mirror, he asked himself if indeed it did come to that, could he actually pull the trigger on the President?

He recalled the times he had acted as the President's personal bodyguard.

No, he had to tell himself. *Anyone else but.*

From the rest room he walked back across the terminal to where he had left Joy. Only she wasn't there.

For a moment he looked around, wondering if he had mistaken the area, but then he spotted Joy's retreating figure moving down the escalator. A tall, husky man dressed in a plain gray suit had hold of her right arm. Another man was below her, and then they disappeared.

Carter raced across the terminal to the escalator and started down, several other people between him and Joy.

At the bottom, he got off just as the two men were hustling Joy toward the main doors out of the terminal. He dropped his suitcase by one of the support columns and sprinted after them.

They were just going out the doors when he came up behind them. He had pulled out his Luger and held it low at his side.

Joy and the man to her right noticed Carter coming up, and they both turned at the same moment.

"Oh!" Joy gasped.

The man grunted and reached inside his coat, but Carter brought up his Luger and jammed it into his side.

"You're a dead man if you don't take your hand away," Carter said softly.

They stopped. The man on Joy's left had spun around and he too reached for his gun, but Carter shook his head.

"Your partner is a dead man the moment I see your weapon," Carter said.

Joy disengaged herself and stepped back. A gray Chevrolet had pulled up to the curb, and the driver was looking at them, his mouth open.

"You have two choices, gentlemen," Carter said. "We can fight it out here, or the three of you can drop your weapons in the back seat of the car and walk away from this in one piece. I don't want this little episode to get messy."

For a second no one said a thing. The windows were down on the car, and the driver had clearly heard everything.

Carter jabbed the man at his side with Wilhelmina.

"All right, we'll do as the man says, nice and easy so no one gets hurt," the driver said.

Carter watched as he pulled out his pistol and dropped it on the floor in the back. He got out of the car and stepped away from it.

"The keys are in the ignition, Carter," he said.

Carter motioned to the other men, who reluctantly pulled out their weapons and dropped them on the back seat. There were hundreds of people around, but no one seemed to notice what was happening.

Joy hurried around to the driver's side and got in behind the wheel. She started the car.

Carter looked at the three men. "Walk. Don't look back. It'll be over in a minute or so, and you can call in the reinforcements."

The three men walked down the sidewalk, and when they were twenty yards away, Carter jumped in the car and Joy took off. Before they got completely around the sweeping curve down to the main airport road, Carter looked back. The three men were running back into the terminal.

Down at the exit, Carter directed Joy to the left instead of to the right.

"That's back to the terminal," she protested.

"Right," Carter said. "Park on the ramp. We're going back to rent a car. We won't get very far in this one."

She saw the logic in that, and she turned left. They went up the ramp, and Joy parked the car in an out-of-the-way corner.

They found the car rental counters, where they signed up for a car. Their destination: Washington, D.C.

While Joy was doing the paperwork, Carter slipped over to the main exits. There was no suspicious activity here, and he easily retrieved his suitcase. The trio probably assumed they were already headed for New York City.

He and Joy went back to where the rental cars were parked, got theirs, and were soon well away from the airport, Carter driving.

They crossed Manhattan, then took Interstate 80 to the west, always staying well within the speed limit, stopping only for gas and something to eat.

Hour by hour, the car they had rented clocked mile after mile. East of Cleveland they headed south on 71 through Columbus, Cincinnati, and Louisville, again turning west on 64.

For a time Joy drove while Carter slept, and always they kept an eye on the rearview mirror. But no one was coming after them.

On the second day they were through St. Louis, Kansas City, and late that night, Denver, where they turned south, going through the mountains into New Mexico and into Arizona. They made it over to Tucson on Interstate 10 by midafternoon.

It was hot, at least a hundred in the shade when they parked behind the Ramada Inn southeast of town. They had passed the Davis-Monthan Air Force Base and the international airport on the way in, but nothing seemed out of the ordinary. Yet Carter could feel that something was happening here. He didn't know exactly what it was, but he just knew that something was going on.

Carter went inside and registered under an assumed name, giving a false license plate number and state. It was something hotel registration clerks never checked.

Once they were in their room, they ordered in an early dinner, and Carter waited for it to come while Joy took a cool shower. He stood by the window looking out across the parking lot, beyond the interstate highway to the desert. It was a forbidding-looking countryside. Very reminiscent of the deserts of Iran and the area around the Dead Sea in Israel.

Joy was finished in the shower and he was taking his when their dinner came. They ate, then crawled into bed, falling asleep instantly. It had been a grueling twenty-five hundred miles from New York, and they were both dead tired. Tonight, there'd be much work to be done.

Carter came straight awake, and he sat up in bed. It was dark, and Joy was gone. The only light came from outside, through the open-weave curtains on the windows facing the parking lot. He held his breath, listening to the lack of sound in the room, the sounds of the motel, and finally the sounds of the trucks rolling by on the highway outside.

He threw back the covers and got out of bed. She wasn't in the bathroom. He flipped on the lights and quickly got dressed, strapping on his weapons. She was gone. She could have gone down to the bar for a drink, or she could have taken off.

Someone was at the door. He stepped back into the bathroom and pulled out his Luger as he flipped off the lights.

A moment later Joy came into the room, locking the door behind her. She looked toward the bed and not seeing Carter, turned suddenly toward the bathroom as he flipped on the lights.

Her face was white, her mouth slightly open, her brown eyes wide. She looked guilty as hell.

''Nick,'' she breathed. ''You scared me.''

Carter stepped out of the bathroom, holstering the Luger. ''I woke up and you were gone.''

''I couldn't sleep . . .''

''Who'd you call?''

''Call . . . ?''

"Joy, who'd you telephone? Who'd you call out here? Langley?"

Her lower lip quivered. She stepped back.

"Shit," he said in disgust. He turned away momentarily, but then he turned back. "I guess I understand." He went to the bureau where he grabbed the car keys. He turned around and tossed them to her. She caught them.

"What's this supposed to mean?" she asked.

"Go on back to Washington. You can tell them you escaped. They'll welcome you with open arms."

"It's not what you think, Nick," she said.

"I want you out of here, Joy," Carter said. "I don't trust you."

For several long moments it seemed as if she were going to challenge him, but then she turned and stormed out of the room, slamming the door behind her.

Carter waited a couple of minutes before he slipped out of the room and took the back stairs down to the rear parking lot, where he held back behind the ice machine.

Joy stood near the car looking up at their room, then she climbed in, started it, and took off.

Carter did not feel bad about her. He understood her loyalties. He felt the same kinds of stirrings. It was very difficult not to go along with whatever was put in front of you by your own government.

He stood there for a very long time. Finally he made his way through the corridors to the front desk, where, despite the hour, he arranged to rent a car and have it delivered within a half hour.

Back in his room, he pocketed his money and passports, then took a deep drink of the cognac they had bought on the trip down.

He telephoned AXE and quickly told the man in Operations what he was going to do, but before the call could be switched to Hawk or before any objections could be raised, he hung up.

Carter sat back in the chair by the window, his eyes half closed. He felt suddenly clean, as if there was nothing to impede his progress, as if there were no reasons for him not to push this thing to the limits. Whatever it came to, he'd definitely push.

At length he went downstairs and made his way to the front desk where he signed some forms, showed his license, and then went outside where he collected his car, a Chevy Citation.

He headed out away from the motel past the Pima County Hospital, then up past Reid Park and out East 22nd Street, finally cutting south again on Wilmont Road.

The last houses were about a half mile from the outer perimeter fence of the air base, which was lit by powerful lights every hundred yards.

Carter parked his car a few blocks from the fence, left the keys beneath the mat, and continued the rest of the way on foot. The night was cool. In the distance to the south he thought he heard a jet take off, but then he wasn't quite sure.

The fence was twelve feet tall and topped with barbed wire. Carter made his way halfway between one set of lights and the next, quickly took off his jacket, and scaled the fence. At the top he threw his jacket over the barbed wire, then climbed over it. On the other side, he carefully disengaged his jacket and climbed down.

At the bottom he put his jacket back on, then headed out across a wide field toward a series of low hills.

Carter had no real idea what he expected to find here, except that whatever had happened in Saudi Arabia led to an abandoned base in Iran, which led to an abandoned base in Israel, which finally led here. The string of leads was ominous. He could do nothing less than follow them.

About three quarters of a mile across the field, the desert land rose gradually up to the crest of a small hill. As Carter topped it, the base suddenly spread out beneath him. Far to the left, running mostly west to east, were the runways. Straight ahead and into the distance to the right were the hangars and maintenance buildings. Beyond were the barracks and other base buildings.

Absolutely nothing looked out of the ordinary. This seemed like any other air base.

Carter crouched on the crest of the hill looking down at the base. The runways and alert hangars would be heavily guarded. The base proper would be open except for routine surveillance.

For just a minute Carter felt foolish sneaking onto the base like this. Nothing was going on here. Absolutely nothing. And when it was all over he'd feel silly about this. But then he thought about the bases in Iran and in Israel. They led here.

He got up and, keeping low, worked his way down the hill to the southwest toward the base proper, away from the runways.

What he wanted to find was the BOQ or perhaps even the operations officer. If he could find some officer, a major or higher, he might be able to sweat something out of him.

Either that or, if this *was* the base from which the strike had originated, there would have to be some sort of a staging area, a special section of the base set apart from everything else. It would probably be somewhere off one of the runways. Or perhaps stuck in some remote corner of the base.

But that too he would get from whatever officer he managed to corner.

It was nearly a mile down the hill, across a long field of scrub and across a wide drainage ditch, to the end of one of the streets that ran from north to south across the base.

The barracks were mostly all dark at this hour of the

morning, but far to the south he could see the lights of the main gate. As he watched, a set of headlights swung down the road, headed toward him, but then turned left.

From the drainage ditch he hurried across the road and slipped into the shadows beside one of the buildings. Again, in the distance, he was certain he could hear a high-flying jet, but then the noise faded.

He made his way around to the front of the building. On a large wooden sign at the corner of the building was the number T301. The next building down the street was numbered T303, the one across the street T302.

These were ordinary barracks, by the looks of them. Behind the buildings were dozens of automobiles parked in wide parking lots. Many of them looked very old and battered. This was enlisted men's territory.

He hurried down the street in the direction of the main gate, constantly watching the road as well as the buildings themselves for any sign that he was being watched. But there continued to be nothing. At length he came to a building whose sign out front said BACHELOR OFFICERS' QUARTERS.

A light was on in one of the rooms on the second floor. Carter hurried around to the back of the building and slipped into the ground-floor corridor.

The building was quiet. The corridor was lit by red fire lights at both exits, as were the stairwells.

He made his way to the second floor and down the corridor to the room with the light shining from beneath the door. Soft strains of classical music came from inside.

Carter pulled out his Luger and tried the doorknob; it was open. He let himself in.

A young man with dark hair, dressed only in his shorts and T-shirt, lay on his bed, a glass of wine on the floor beside him, listening to what sounded like Tchaikovsky.

He jumped up, knocking over the wine when he saw Carter and the gun in his hand.

"My God!" he cried. "Oh . . . my . . . God." He raised his hands over his head.

"Who are you?" Carter asked.

"Sir . . . I . . ."

"Your name and rank and duty section," Carter snapped. Christ, he hated this.

"Hubert, sir. Lieutenant Robert J."

Damn, Carter thought.

"Is this a robbery?"

"I'm looking for the base commander."

"Sir?"

"Your base commander!" Carter repeated. "Does he reside on base?"

"No, sir."

"Then how about the commander of your special section? Does he reside on base?"

"Yes, sir . . ." the lieutenant started to say, but then he cut it off.

"Thank you, son," Carter said. The lieutenant's trousers were draped over a chair. Carter went across the room, grabbed them, and tossed them across. "Get dressed, Robert J., we're going out."

For a moment the young lieutenant hesitated. Carter slowly and deliberately raised the Luger and pointed it at the man, his stomach turning over at what he was doing.

The lieutenant turned white and hurried to put on his trousers. Carter threw him his shirt and shoved his shoes across.

When he was dressed, Carter stepped aside and motioned toward the door.

"Where are we going? What do you want?"

"We've going to pay a visit to the commander of the special section on this base."

"I don't know what you're talking about, sir."

"The section that trained with the half-track vehicles out in the desert and the C-130s for touch-and-go landings. *That* special section," Carter said.

"Oh, God," the lieutenant said. "I knew it. I just knew it would come to this."

At the same moment that Carter noticed the chaplain's insignia on the young man's uniform collar, the base siren started wailing.

FIFTEEN

"Have you got a car, Chaplain?" Carter asked, lowering his Luger.

"It's Father, and yes I do," the lieutenant said.

"You can lower your hands. I couldn't shoot you if I had to."

The priest brought his arms to his sides. "What is this all about?" he asked. He had cocked his head and was listening to the siren. "Has it something to do with that?"

"If that's coming from your special section, yes, probably. A friend of mine, a young woman who works for the Central Intelligence Agency, has probably set off the alarm. She'll be in trouble now."

"And do you work for the . . . CIA?"

"No," Carter said. "But I do work for the government."

"Why are you here?"

Carter took a deep breath and let it out slowly as he holstered Wilhelmina. "It has to do with the nuclear strike on Saudi Arabia. I believe the unit that made the strike is or was based here. I've come to put an end to it."

"Then it is true after all," the priest murmured.

"What is, Father? What do you know?"

The priest blinked, and he shook his head. "Nothing,

really, mostly just suspicions some of us had. There was training here in what you call a 'special section.' It's the 738th Army Airborne Wing. They were brought down here for special training. All of them were so . . . different, including their commander, Colonel Hardesty.''

''C-130s? Half-track vehicles?''

''For months out in the fields north of the alert pods,'' the priest said. ''They were apart. They even had their own section of the base, fenced off from the rest of us.''

''Are they still here?'' Carter asked.

''They left two weeks before the . . . nuclear strike.''

''Then they're not here?''

The priest blinked. ''Oh, they're here. At least some of them are. They came back two days ago.'' Again the priest cocked his head toward the siren. ''That siren is coming from their section over by what used to be our motor pool.''

Joy, Carter thought. He grabbed the priest by the arm.

''You're going to have to drive me over there, show me where Colonel Hardesty's quarters are.''

''No . . . I . . .'' the young priest mumbled, but then he straightened up. ''If they did this thing . . . if they . . .'' He grabbed his hat and his car keys, and led Carter downstairs to the back parking lot where they climbed into an old Volkswagen.

''We have to hurry, Father,'' Carter said, and as they pulled out of the parking lot the siren suddenly stopped. The silence was ominous.

''Oh, dear,'' the priest said.

There were a lot of lights around four buildings that were surrounded by a tall, temporary-looking fence. Signs warning of high voltage were wired to the fence every fifty or seventy-five feet.

At least a couple of hundred officers and men were gathered across the street from an open gate in the fence where an ambulance was parked, its red lights flashing. There were a lot of military police jeeps there, and just through the gate, at the front of the ambulance, was a knot of officers.

"There he is," the priest said, pulling up.

"Which one?" Carter asked.

"The gray-haired man. In the middle. That's Colonel Hardesty."

"Thank you, Father," Carter said. He pulled out his Luger and, holding it out of sight at his side, worked his way through the crowd.

"Step aside, I'm a doctor. Step aside," Carter said. He hurried across the street once he was clear of the crowd, and several MPs turned to challenge him. "I'm a doctor," Carter shouted. "Let me through!"

They parted, and he was through the gate and around to the front of the ambulance.

They were just putting a sheet over Joy Makepiece's blackened face. She had evidently tried to make it over the fence and had hit the high voltage. The stench of cooked flesh was still strong.

"Hey, he's got a gun," someone shouted as Carter came up to Colonel Hardesty.

The colonel, a craggy-faced man in his mid-forties with short-cropped gray hair, spun around, then reached for the .45 at his hip, but Carter was at his side and had jammed the Luger into the man's ribs before he got the gun.

"You're dead, Hardesty, if you don't do exactly as I say."

Hardesty stared at him. Carter pressed the Luger's muzzle into his side with a little more force.

"I've come too far to stop now."

The military policemen, their weapons drawn, were staring at them.

"What do you want?"

"Is there a helicopter here? Within your little compound."

"Yes," Hardesty said tensely.

"Good. We're going to step back away from the gate. We're going to call for a pilot, and we're getting out of here."

"Where are you taking me? And who the hell are you?"

"Where you're going depends totally on you, Colonel. Let's move it."

Hardesty looked up and waved the others away. "He has a gun in my ribs. We're taking my helicopter out of here. Call my pilot, Captain Johns. Get him over to the chopper immediately."

They backed slowly away from the ambulance and from Joy's body lying beneath the sheet on the stretcher. What the hell had she been doing here? The only thing Carter could figure was that she had hoped to provide him with a diversion, just as he had for her back at the soccer stadium in Riyadh. He felt very bad for her and for the things he had said to her. But it needn't have come to this.

He and the colonel made it around the corner of the old motor pool building, out of sight of the others.

"Where is it?" Carter asked.

"In back."

"Let's go," Carter said, hustling Hardesty along.

"Who are you? What the hell do you want here?"

"I'm Nick Carter."

Hardesty half turned to look back at Carter. "Oh," he said. "It's you. I should have known after Riyadh, Bandar Ma'Shur, and Mār Sābā."

"How'd you know I was there?"

Hardesty laughed. "Military intelligence, how else? And do you actually think you're going to get away with anything? You can't stop it, you know. It's already grown too big. Before too long it'll come out about the cooperation we had with General David Goldman."

"Israeli Army?"

"Air Force, and his chief of staff, and several other officers who arranged for us to use Mār Sābā."

"And there'll be Iranian government cooperation?"

"Their Air Force as well," Hardesty said, and he laughed. "It's gone too far. It'll all come out, and it'll be war in the Middle East."

They made it around the corner to the helicopter as a jeep came from the other direction and pulled up. An officer jumped out but stopped short when he saw Hardesty and Carter.

"My pilot," Hardesty said.

"Tell him to get the chopper started. We're leaving immediately."

"We're getting out of here, Bob. He's got a gun, so for the time being let's go along with him."

For several long seconds the captain stood rooted to his spot.

"Move it, Bob. He's got a gun!" Hardesty shouted.

"They found out he was coming, Colonel," the captain said.

"What are you talking about?"

"I was coming to tell you. It just came in over the crypto circuit." The captain looked at Carter. "You're Carter, aren't you? And the woman was Joy Makepiece? CIA?"

"That's right," Carter said.

"What's going on?" Hardesty demanded, sweat pouring down the side of his face.

"It's General Richardson, sir."

"What about him?"

"He said it was over. He had done what he could, but now it was over. Too many people were finding out—even the President would know. Even the President, Colonel. Which meant I was right. Oh, Christ . . ."

"What has happened, you bastard? Tell me!"

"It's General Richardson. He committed suicide in his office in the Pentagon not more than half an hour ago."

"No!" Hardesty shouted, and he shoved Carter backward and started for the helicopter.

Carter regained his balance, brought up the Luger with both hands, and fired two shots, both of them hitting the colonel in the neck.

The captain had dropped into a crouch, clutching his own gun, but when he saw that the colonel was dead, he uncocked the automatic and shoved it back in his holster. Then he turned to Carter.

"Mr. Carter, there is someone on the encrypted teletype circuit who wishes urgently to speak with you."

Slowly Carter straightened up, and he holstered his Luger. Several military police jeeps and a dozen armed men all raced back from the front of the compound as Captain Johns stepped across to where Carter stood motionless.

"It's all right!" the captain shouted. "It's all right! Get an ambulance back here—the Colonel has been hurt."

There was a lot of confusion for at least ten minutes before Carter and Captain Johns were allowed to get back to the communications center. The captain left Carter there with the encrypted telephone.

"Hello," he said tiredly. He could not get Joy out of his mind.

"Hello, Nick." Hawk's voice came over the secured line. "Have you heard about Richardson?"

"Just now, sir," Carter said. "He masterminded the entire thing?"

"Apparently."

"How did he get past the Joint Chiefs?"

"He didn't. As soon as it happened, he was the one taking over the secret investigation. Meanwhile, they were preparing for the war."

"War?"

"That's what he wanted, as far as we can tell. The information is just now coming in, so it's still not perfectly clear, but apparently the general felt that the only way to secure our oil interests in the Middle East against Soviet encroachment was to start a war there between Saudi Arabia and Israel."

"I don't see . . ."

"A nuclear war that would demand our immediate intervention. Once we had the territory, we'd never let it go."

It was clear then. "I see, sir," Carter said. "But he didn't think he could get away with it. Under the noses of the Joint Chiefs, under the President's nose."

"He nearly did, Nick. He very nearly did."

EPILOGUE

It had been a terribly confusing two weeks since Tucson, Nick Carter thought as his flight came in for a graceful landing at the Nice airport on the Côte d'Azur, but finally the world was coming back into focus.

The public, of course, had heard very little of what actually happened, but in very high levels of government apologies were made, reparations payments were arranged, and gradually the tense situation in the Middle East began to calm down.

Even the Russians, who everyone thought would naturally make a great deal out of the situation, were strangely silent. Only a short story in *Izvestia* mentioned an American grant of $4.5 billion to help Saudi Arabia recover its oil revenue losses.

The Israelis were far too embarrassed about their unwitting participation in the business to say anything publicly, and of course no one believed anything the Khoumeni government said. So the dust had begun to settle.

Very quietly the President was ramrodding a few new laws through Congress, giving more civilian control over the military. He had fired the secretary of defense, and in the

Pentagon there was a major shakeup of personnel that would be going on for at least the next year.

We had come close to all-out war this time. The public in general would never know about it, which was just as well. But it was frightening that it had very nearly happened.

Marie Arlemont, wearing a light gauze shirt over very tight jeans, was waiting at the terminal when Carter stepped off the jet. She had learned a few of the details of the incident through her connection with the SDECE, and she was immediately solicitous, taking him by the arm and talking incessantly as she led him out to her Ferrari.

Carter finally stopped her prattling. "Marie," he said, putting down his suitcase and taking her hands.

She blinked but swallowed her next words.

"I'm on vacation. I don't give a damn what happened or what will happen to the world. For the next ten days I want to do nothing more than eat, sleep, lie around the beach, and . . ."

"Make love with me," Marie said, her eyes twinkling.

"And make love with you," Carter agreed.

She reached into the car and pulled out a chilled bottle of champagne. "Do the honors?" she asked. He took the bottle and opened it, the cork flying, champagne foam bubbling all over the place, as she got the glasses.

It would be nice if the only explosions on this earth were those of popping champagne corks, Carter thought as they clinked glasses. And they drank the icy wine beneath the hot Mediterranean sun and thought only of what future days, and nights, would bring.

DON'T MISS THE NEXT NEW
NICK CARTER SPY THRILLER

OPERATION SHARKBITE

Carter crouched in the closet, the scent from Bridgit Michaels's clothing filling his nostrils. The sap he had almost used on the shooter at Grayburn House was in his right hand.

Just in case, Wilhelmina occupied his left.

No lights were on in the living room or the bedroom. A narrow shaft of sunlight seeped through a crack in the drapes to fall across the hanks of hair on the pillow and the sheet covering the wadded blankets serving as bodies.

The door from the living room to the bedroom was open about six inches and within Carter's sight.

It had been about ten minutes since Bridgit had done her towel-waving routine from the front window. Now she was dressed and crouching on the fire escape outside the window.

"What if the neighbors across the way see me?" she had asked.

"Wave to 'em. You're just getting some early morning air."

For ten seconds and ten seconds only, Carter had thought about calling Hamilton and MI5 for backup. But if there was another leak in MI5 besides Bridgit, it would do little good . . . and maybe blow the whole thing.

A creak of wood . . . faint, barely discernible . . . but there.

It was the front door of the flat.

Carter tensed, relaxed, and tensed his muscles again to get them ready.

The bedroom door moved an inch, and then another six inches.

The first thing through the opening was the silenced snout of a Heckler and Koch UP70 machine pistol. Like everything else the West Germans manufactured, the UP70 was a work of art.

It operated on selective three round bursts from an eighteen round feeder, at a deadly cyclic rate of 2,200 rounds per minute.

Just as fast as the trigger could be pulled.

The man behind the UP70 was young, wearing jeans and a baggy pullover. The sweater had probably been used to hide the machine pistol as he crossed the street and climbed the stairs to 3C.

His all-night vigil showed. His lean, deeply tanned face badly needed a shave.

He moved toward the bed with startling economy. So much so that it seemed that no part of him moved except the extended arm holding the pistol.

When the hand holding the UP70 was just over the foot-board of the bed, the long silencer began bucking. The room was filled with the smell of burnt powder and the dull thud of the slugs as they tore into the heavy blankets.

Nick Carter was a pro. He recognized another one.

The guy took no chances. He just kept firing.

Carter counted the bursts in his head: four . . . five . . . six.

Three times six is eighteen; exactly what the UP70 magazine held.

The shooter was just moving around the bed on Carter's side to check his handiwork when the Killmaster moved out.

The guy was sharp.

Carter's gliding steps barely made a sound on the rug, but he heard them.

—From OPERATION SHARKBITE
A New Nick Carter Spy Thriller
From Charter in April

☐ 08374-9	**THE BUDAPEST RUN**	$2.50
☐ 14217-6	**THE DEATH DEALER**	$2.50
☐ 14220-6	**DEATH ISLAND**	$2.50
☐ 14172-2	**THE DEATH STAR AFFAIR**	$2.50
☐ 14221-4	**THE DECOY HIT**	$2.50
☐ 17014-5	**THE DUBROVNIK MASSACRE**	$2.25
☐ 18102-3	**EARTHFIRE NORTH**	$2.50
☐ 29782-X	**THE GOLDEN BULL**	$2.25
☐ 33068-1	**HIDE AND GO DIE**	$2.50
☐ 34909-9	**THE HUMAN TIME BOMB**	$2.25
☐ 34999-4	**THE HUNTER**	$2.50
☐ 35868-3	**THE INCA DEATH SQUAD**	$2.50
☐ 37484-0	**THE INSTABUL DECISION**	$2.50
☐ 47183-8	**THE LAST SUMARAI**	$2.50
☐ 57502-1	**NIGHT OF THE WARHEADS**	$2.50
☐ 58866-2	**NORWEGIAN TYPHOON**	$2.50
☐ 63430-3	**OPERATION VENDETTA**	$2.50
☐ 65176-3	**THE PARISIAN AFFAIR**	$2.50
☐ 67081-4	**PLEASURE ISLAND**	$2.50
☐ 71133-2	**THE REDOLMO AFFAIR**	$1.95
☐ 71228-2	**THE REICH FOUR**	$1.95
☐ 95305-0	**THE YUKON TARGET**	$2.50

Prices may be slightly higher in Canada.

Available at your local bookstore or return this form to:

CHARTER BOOKS
Book Mailing Service
P.O. Box 690, Rockville Centre, NY 11571

Please send me the titles checked above. I enclose _____ Include 75¢ for postage and handling if one book is ordered; 25¢ per book for two or more not to exceed $1.75. California, Illinois, New York and Tennessee residents please add sales tax.

NAME _____

ADDRESS _____

CITY _____ STATE/ZIP _____

(allow six weeks for delivery.)

☐ 71539-7	**RETREAT FOR DEATH**	$2.50
☐ 75035-4	**THE SATAN TRAP**	$1.95
☐ 76347-2	**THE SIGN OF THE COBRA**	$2.25
☐ 77193-9	**THE SNAKE FLAG CONSPIRACY**	$2.25
☐ 77413-X	**SOLAR MENACE**	$2.50
☐ 79073-9	**THE STRONTIUM CODE**	$2.50
☐ 79077-1	**THE SUICIDE SEAT**	$2.25
☐ 81025-X	**TIME CLOCK OF DEATH**	$1.75
☐ 82407-2	**TRIPLE CROSS**	$1.95
☐ 82726-8	**TURKISH BLOODBATH**	$2.25
☐ 87192-5	**WAR FROM THE CLOUDS**	$2.25
☐ 01276-0	**THE ALGARVE AFFAIR**	$2.50
☐ 09157-1	**CARIBBEAN COUP**	$2.50
☐ 63424-9	**OPERATION SHARKBITE**	$2.50
☐ 95935-0	**ZERO-HOUR STRIKE FORCE**	$2.50

Available at your local bookstore or return this form to:

 CHARTER BOOKS
Book Mailing Service
P.O. Box 690, Rockville Centre, NY 11571

Please send me the titles checked above. I enclose _____. Include 75¢ for postage and handling if one book is ordered; 25¢ per book for two or more not to exceed $1.75. California, Illinois, New York and Tennessee residents please add sales tax.

NAME_____

ADDRESS_____

CITY_____STATE/ZIP_____

(allow six weeks for delivery.)   A8